SPECIAL MESSAGE TO READERS

THE ULVERSCROFT FOUNDATION
(registered UK charity number 264873)
was established in 1972 to provide funds for research, diagnosis and treatment of eye diseases. Examples of major projects funded by the Ulverscroft Foundation are:-

- The Children's Eye Unit at Moorfields Eye Hospital, London
- The Ulverscroft Children's Eye Unit at Great Ormond Street Hospital for Sick Children
- Funding research into eye diseases and treatment at the Department of Ophthalmology, University of Leicester
- The Ulverscroft Vision Research Group, Institute of Child Health
- Twin operating theatres at the Western Ophthalmic Hospital, London
- The Chair of Ophthalmology at the Royal Australian College of Ophthalmologists

You can help further the work of the Foundation by making a donation or leaving a legacy. Every contribution is gratefully received. If you would like to help support the Foundation or require further information, please contact:

THE ULVERSCROFT FOUNDATION
The Green, Bradgate Road, Anstey
Leicester LE7 7FU, England
Tel: (0116) 236 4325

website: www.foundation.ulverscroft.com

WEDDING BELLS

Marina is attending her widowed father's wedding when she is immediately drawn to handsome fellow guest Roberto. A romance soon sparks between them, but it's anything but smooth sailing ahead when Marina discovers her old flame, Jon, has lost his memory, and visits him in hospital. Torn between trying to help him and spending time with her new love, Marina is distraught. Can she and Roberto overcome their difficulties and find happiness together?

DAWN BRIDGE

WEDDING BELLS

Complete and Unabridged

LINFORD
Leicester

First published in Great Britain in 2015

First Linford Edition
published 2016

*A catalogue record for this book is available
from the British Library.*

ISBN 978–1–4448–3053–8

Published by
F. A. Thorpe (Publishing)
Anstey, Leicestershire

Set by Words & Graphics Ltd.
Anstey, Leicestershire
Printed and bound in Great Britain by
T. J. International Ltd., Padstow, Cornwall

This book is printed on acid-free paper

1

'We are gathered here together to celebrate the marriage of this man and this woman . . . ' the registrar's voice droned on.

Marina gazed around the elegant hall, noting the happy, smiling faces, before briefly focussing her attention on the couple who were standing, hand in hand, beneath a sumptuous glass chandelier. Then she looked down at her service sheet, no longer hearing the words, as memories came flooding back. Not for the first time, Marina asked herself what she was doing here.

'You're my only daughter,' Lionel had said. 'You have to come.'

He was right of course, Marina reflected. She had to come, even though she disapproved and felt her father was making a big mistake. He'd have been so disappointed if she'd stayed away from his wedding. Everyone would have wondered why she wasn't there. What reason could she have given for not attending? That she thought her dad had made a bad choice? That he was being disloyal to the memory of her mother? No, those excuses wouldn't be acceptable. It was up to him what he did now, and who he chose for his wife. Was she just jealous that she would no longer be the main focus of his attention? Whatever her motives, Marina knew she had to accept his decision.

Marina thought back over the past three years since her mother had died. She and her father had kept in close contact — until recently, when suddenly he'd become quite secretive. He'd stopped answering her telephone calls, rarely sent texts and had seldom come round to see her. Although they worked in the same company, they only seemed to glimpse each other in passing, rarely getting a chance to say more than a few words.

This was unusual, so when she'd finally managed to corner him, she asked him straight out: 'What's going on, Dad?'

'Nothing. I've been extremely busy at work recently. And I've been having trouble with my mobile,' came his reply.

This hadn't satisfied Marina, but she'd kept quiet, thinking he probably wanted to be more independent and build a new life for himself.

Then, one evening, he'd turned up at her flat unexpectedly.

'Come in, Dad. What a lovely surprise,' Marina said. 'I haven't seen much of you recently.'

'No. I . . . I've been rather busy but . . . there's something I need to tell you.'

'Okay. I was just making a coffee. Would you like one?'

'That would be lovely.'

'Sit down. Make yourself comfortable. I won't be long. Then we can have a nice chat.'

Marina walked into the kitchen,

wondering what her father had to say. He looked quite serious. She hoped it wasn't bad news. Surely he wasn't ill? She couldn't face that again. It had taken her all this time to come to terms with what had happened to her mother. But her dad had never been ill in his life. It couldn't be that, could it?

A few minutes later, Marina had made the drinks and they were sitting opposite one another.

'Now, what have you got to tell me?' she enquired tentatively.

'I . . . ' He hesitated, then blurted out, 'I've met a wonderful woman and . . . we're going to get married.'

'You're . . . ?' Marina stared at him, speechless. She'd never envisaged this happening. She banged her coffee cup clumsily onto the table, spilling some of the contents.

'I'm getting married,' he repeated.

'Married! When? Who?' She was too stunned to say anything more intelligible.

'She's called Amelia. You'll love her

when you meet her.'

Marina was sure she wouldn't.

'And it's happening next month,' her father continued.

'Next month?' Marina gaped, open-mouthed, at her father. Now she knew why her dad was never at home when she called.

'Yes. The hotel's booked, it's all arranged. The marriage ceremony will take place during the afternoon. Then, after that, we'll have the wedding breakfast in the private restaurant, followed by dancing in the adjoining ballroom.'

'Where's it going to be held?'

'Green Lawns Hotel, just up the road from you. Have you been inside? It's a really beautiful place. Ideal for a summer wedding. There are several function rooms scattered around the extensive grounds.'

'You sound like a tour guide.'

'I'm just answering your question. Oh, Marina, don't look so shocked,' Lionel said. 'It's not that bad. You must

5

have known it might happen one day. Aren't you going to congratulate me?'

'Yes, I suppose so. I just wasn't expecting it now. You could have given me some warning.' Marina found her voice again. 'Why so soon? Don't you think you're rushing things, Dad? You can hardly know her, surely. Why not wait a while? See how things go.'

'I knew, the moment I met Amelia, she was the one for me. The same as it was when I saw your mother all those years ago. It will happen to you one day,' her father had assured her.

'I don't think that's very likely,' she'd retorted. She'd never had those feelings for anyone.

'That's because you haven't met the right man. But when you do, you'll feel the same way.'

Marina didn't believe in all that romantic nonsense, but she knew there was no point in arguing with her father. He could be very stubborn, and now he'd made up his mind to marry Amelia, Marina knew there was nothing she could do about it.

'You can bring someone with you to the ceremony,' Lionel told her. 'Any boyfriends on the scene?'

Not now Jon's in Australia, she thought to herself.

'No, nobody,' she replied.

'You can bring a friend, then.'

'No, I'll come on my own.'

'Well, it's up to you, but if you change your mind you'll have to let me know quickly, because of the catering arrangements.'

'I won't change my mind,' Marina said, snappishly.

'Okay. Don't bite my head off.'

'Sorry.' She spoke more quietly. 'So, how did you meet Amelia?'

'On holiday.'

'A holiday romance!' Marina said, scornfully. Now it all fell into place. That had been the point at which he'd become more elusive — since returning from his holiday. He'd been busy with his new girlfriend, and she'd suspected nothing.

'Please try to be happy for me,' Lionel begged. 'I know I'm doing the right thing. And I hope you and Amelia will become the best of friends.'

Marina doubted that. She felt upset that her father could even consider replacing her mother with another woman. Surely it was just an infatuation? A suspicion popped into her head.

'Was it a singles holiday?'

'Yes, it was.'

'I thought as much.'

'What does that mean?'

'A lot of single women, all trying to grab a man — especially one who looks as if he has some money.'

'It wasn't like that. You're so cynical, Marina.'

'I'm only thinking about you. Are you sure you know what you're letting yourself in for?'

'Quite sure.'

In the time that had passed between that conversation and the wedding, Marina had met Amelia just once. The happy couple had called in on their way to the theatre.

Marina had to admit that Amelia was very attractive — quite beautiful in fact — and that she had been pleasant and friendly towards her; but her overriding impression was that Amelia looked much too young for her father.

'I'm pleased to meet you at last,' Amelia had said. 'I've heard so much about you. Your father is very proud of how you coped and looked after him when your mother passed away, you know.'

Marina could think of no reply to that, other than the obligatory 'Pleased to meet you, too.' She'd had no choice but to cope, her father had been in such a state of anguish. Marina tried to make her words sound sincere, but she really wasn't pleased to meet Amelia. She guessed, too, that Amelia could sense her coolness and was trying to win her round.

Marina was convinced it would all end in disaster. She hoped she was wrong, but feared she wasn't. Later, when she'd seen her father on his own, she'd asked, 'How old is Amelia?'

'Older than you'd think,' was her father's reply.

Marina wondered why her dad had to make such a mystery of everything.

'So, what age is that?' she persisted.

There was a pause.

'Thirty-five.'

'So, you're fifteen years older than her.'

'Yes. Does that matter?' he asked, defensively.

'No, I suppose not.'

As much as she hoped it was not the case, she couldn't help wondering if Amelia was more interested in Lionel's money than in him. After all, he was a wealthy man, on the board of directors of a successful advertising agency. She tried once again to advise caution.

'Why don't you wait just a little longer to get married? You haven't known Amelia very long. Why are you rushing it?'

'Look, Marina, it's all settled. We're adults; we know what we want. Waiting a while won't make any difference. We're not going to change our minds. I'm sorry you're finding this so hard. I never expected that.'

'I'm sorry, Dad. I don't want to upset you, but . . . '

Marina stalled, and Lionel jumped in.

'When your Mum died, I didn't think I would ever get married again; I wasn't interested. But then I met Amelia, and everything changed in a flash. Can't you please just try to be happy for me?'

Marina felt terrible. She didn't want to spoil things for her father, but she couldn't get these niggling doubts out of her head.

'I will. I'll try,' she promised. 'It's just been something of a shock, that's all.'

'I can understand you were surprised by my news, but there's no need for you to have such a tragic look on your face,' Lionel smiled. 'We're planning a wedding, not a funeral! Everything's going

11

to be all right, you'll see.'

Marina hoped he was right. She wondered what her mother would have thought about it. Would she have wanted Lionel to get married again? Marina had never asked that question. Her parents had been such a devoted couple that she'd not even considered the possibility; no man could have done more for his wife than her father had for her mother throughout her two year illness. How could he want to start afresh with someone else?

*   *   *

Now, Marina was at the wedding ceremony, finding it hard to concentrate on proceedings. Poems had been read, music played, but she'd heard none of it. She knew only a handful of the guests, and was not looking forward to the reception afterwards.

Marina's parents had been only children, and both sets of grandparents were deceased, so Marina was Lionel's only relative. She recognised a few of her father's work colleagues, but most of the other people here were friends or relations of Amelia.

She shifted on her hard, uncomfortable seat, reminiscent of the pews she had sat on in Sunday School, many years ago, and recalled those last, dreadful days before her mother passed away. Suddenly, her mother's words came back to her, words which had surprised her at the time.

'Your dad is a wonderful man, Marina. I want him to be happy when I'm gone.'

So maybe that answered her question; her mother would have wanted Lionel to marry again. Marina felt a little better. She'd try to enjoy herself and forget all her worries. After all, this was Dad's big day. She couldn't spoil it for him.

She glanced up from her service sheet and became aware of a dark-haired man in the row opposite, gazing across at her. She averted her eyes and smoothed her peach skirt down over her knees. She wondered who this good-looking guest was, but decided it was pointless speculating about him; anyone that stunning must be spoken for. Then she reprimanded herself. She was at her father's wedding — her mind should be on him, not on some handsome stranger.

A few moments later, Marina looked surreptitiously across at him again, and noticed he was sitting between an elderly couple. So he hadn't come with his girlfriend or wife, she realised. Maybe the elderly couple were his parents. Perhaps they were Amelia's aunt and uncle, so he must be a cousin.

He moved slightly on his seat and Marina quickly looked away, her face flushing. What was the matter with her? She didn't usually take so much notice of strange men — but then, she didn't often see anyone as attractive as him. It was probably because she was at a wedding; she was getting silly, romantic ideas. Forget about him, she told herself. Concentrate on Dad.

Finally the service was over; Lionel and Amelia were married, and everyone was outside, throwing confetti and congratulating the newly-weds. She could hear the sound of bells pealing out from the building where the service had been held. It reminded Marina once again of when she'd been a child and attended Sunday School regularly.

Lionel had told her, 'Amelia loves to hear church bells, so we've arranged for the sound of wedding bells to be piped out from the hall.'

Marina had thought if that was the case, why didn't they just get married in church? Then they could have heard genuine wedding bells. However, she'd kept quiet, thinking that what they chose to do was of no concern to her. But she decided that if she ever got married, she would like to have genuine church bells at her wedding.

People were standing around as the photographer took endless shots of the bride and groom. Marina stood at the side, watching. She wondered idly if she ever would get married. She'd had several boyfriends, but only one had been serious — and now he was thousands of miles away. She'd been with him for about a year, and had been shocked when he told her he'd been offered a position at his bank in Australia.

'Why don't you come with me?' Jon had suggested. 'I'm sure you could find a job out there. It would be a great adventure.'

'But Australia's so far away,' she protested. 'Besides, I couldn't leave Dad. He wouldn't be able to cope without me. I'm all he's got. What about your family, don't they mind?'

'Not at all. They think it's a great opportunity. Your dad would get used to it, Marina. You could email or Skype him regularly, and maybe he could even come out to see us.'

She shook her head.

'I can't do it,' she'd said, tearfully. 'But I'll miss you, Jon.'

'I'll miss you too, but I'll keep in touch,' he promised.

Soon after that, Jon had gone alone. Marina had been very upset at the time, but not heartbroken. She realised that although she had been fond of him, she'd never been passionately in love.

All this seemed rather ironic now, especially as Lionel and Amelia were intending to put Lionel's house up for sale as soon as they returned from their honeymoon, and move further out, into a more rural area.

'You won't mind us moving away, will you?' Lionel had asked, anxiously. 'Amelia has this dream of living in the country. You're always busy with your friends, and I'll still see you at work, of course.'

'No, that's all right,' Marina replied. 'And as you say, I'll still see you at work.' There was nothing else she could have said. It seemed that whatever Amelia wanted, her father would give her.

Marina worked in the same company

as her father. He'd been instrumental in getting her a job after she'd left university and moved back home. Her mother had been very ill at the time, and Marina had accepted the position eagerly, as it was quite close to where they lived. She didn't have to spend long travelling, which gave her more time to devote to her parents.

After her mother's death, Marina had worked her way up in the company, until she had a secure, well-paid position and was able to afford the rent on a flat close by.

At first, her father hadn't been happy about her moving out, but in the end he'd agreed.

'I mustn't be selfish,' he'd said. 'You've got to lead your own life. I shouldn't monopolise you.'

Marina maintained a comfortable lifestyle and, as had been the case in her childhood, she lacked nothing. But she couldn't help wondering if she should have gone to Australia with Jon after all. At the very least, it would have been an interesting experience. Whether it would have led to a more permanent relationship, who knew — but certainly, if she had realised that the imminent future held a second marriage for her father, she would have considered Jon's offer more carefully. It was too late now though; Jon was settled in his job at the bank and enjoying life. She'd had an opportunity to see a bit more of the world, and had missed it.

Now Amelia had come onto the scene, Marina felt she was being pushed out by her, and that her father was trying to replace her mother with this new young woman. Marina knew she was probably being irrational, but couldn't help herself.

'Don't they look happy?' An elderly lady nudged Marina back into the present. 'You're Lionel's daughter, aren't you?'

'Yes, that's right.'

'I'm Amelia's Aunt Betty. I'm so pleased for them. I guess you are too.'

'Er . . . yes.'

'It must have been terrible for Lionel, being widowed so young,' Betty went on. 'And for you, of course, losing your mother.'

'It was.'

'I'm sure Amelia will make Lionel very happy. She's a lovely girl, so beautiful in that lace wedding dress, don't you think? Just like a film star,' Betty smiled.

'She is.' Marina couldn't say anything else. It was true, Amelia was extremely attractive.

'Of course, being her auntie, I'm biased.' Betty looked up at Marina, who towered above her. 'You're a pretty girl too, tall and slim. I don't suppose it will be long before someone snaps you up.'

Marina couldn't help smiling. 'I'm not so sure about that,' she replied.

Betty sighed. 'I wasn't that lucky. Not good-looking enough, I suppose. Too short and dumpy. Didn't meet the right man. Still, I've got to eighty-five and

I'm still going strong, so I mustn't grumble.'

Their conversation was interrupted by the photographer.

'Can everyone gather round, please? I need all the members of the bride and groom's family over here so I can take some pictures.'

'That's us,' said Betty.

'Marina, come here,' Lionel called. 'I need a bit of support. You're the only relative I have! Don't stand there all on your own. I want you in the picture.'

'All right,' she replied, as she tiptoed across the grass to stand beside him, regretting the heels on her beautiful, but rather uncomfortable, new shoes.

'You look gorgeous, Marina. Like a bride yourself, in that peach suit,' Lionel whispered.

'Oh, Dad, you do exaggerate!' She blushed, but felt pleased that he appreciated the effort she'd made. 'You don't look too bad, either,' she whispered back.

A group of people — Amelia's

relatives, she presumed — assembled around the bride and groom.

'Smile, everyone,' the photographer urged.

As Marina looked towards the photographer, she noticed that the good-looking man and the elderly couple were standing opposite them, observing the proceedings. Not relatives of Amelia after all, Marina thought. She wondered who they could be. Friends, she supposed. He looked to be about the same age as Amelia.

More pictures were taken, and then the rest of the wedding guests were asked to join them for a group photograph.

Finally, after taking several more shots, the photographer thanked everyone and dismissed them. All the guests started drifting towards the hotel building, where the reception was due to take place. Marina, too, was heading in the same direction, teetering on her high heels, when she tripped over a tree stump. She floundered, and let out a cry, thinking that she was going to fall flat on her face in the grass.

Suddenly, she felt strong arms grabbing her, pulling her upright. Someone had saved her. She looked up into the eyes of the tall, good-looking, young man.

2

'Steady on there! I've got you,' the young man said, as he held onto Marina's shoulders. He looked her up and down. 'We don't want you falling over and ruining your outfit. Those heels aren't exactly suitable for walking on uneven grass, are they?'

'Thank you. I'm all right,' Marina replied curtly, trying to pull herself away from his firm grip. She felt stupid for tripping up, and silently chastised herself for not having been more careful. This stranger didn't need to tell her that high heels were not very practical. She knew that! But they were pretty, matched her suit perfectly, and were just right for a wedding.

'I think I'd better hold onto you until we get onto firmer ground,' he stated.

'That won't be necessary, thank you,'

she answered primly, yanking her arm away.

She stepped forward gingerly, but as her foot touched the ground, she winced with pain.

'Ooh, my ankle!'

'Actually, I think it is necessary,' he said. 'Don't argue. Take my arm. I'll help you. There's a bench over there. We can sit down and see what damage you've done.'

Marina had no choice but to allow him to help her. She felt so embarrassed, and she didn't want to make any more of a scene — people were already beginning to look at them.

The elderly couple she had seen him with earlier were coming towards them, speaking excitedly to each other in a language Marina didn't understand. The young man replied with equally unintelligible words and waved them both away, but the older man patted Marina on the arm, and said, in perfect English, 'Don't worry, dear. You'll be all right; Roberto will take care of you.'

'Thanks, Dad,' the young man replied, brusquely. 'We'll manage. Go and find somewhere for Mum to sit down. I'll see you later.'

He turned to Marina and asked, 'Now, are you going to do as I say?'

'I suppose I'll have to.' She looked up at him. He may have been attractive, but he was also irritatingly self-important!

'I'm just trying to help, you know,' he said, mildly. 'You don't need to glare at me like that.'

She hadn't been aware she was glaring. 'Sorry,' she muttered. 'I just don't want to be a nuisance.'

'You're not, and you don't need to apologise,' he said. 'Let's try to get you sorted out as best we can. Then you'll be able to join in the festivities. You don't want to miss your dad's reception.'

Her father would be wondering where she had got to, that much was true.

'How do you know I'm Lionel's

daughter?' she asked.

'It didn't take much detective work to figure that out. I saw you standing next to him when the photos were being taken.'

Now she felt silly for asking. She took hold of Roberto's arm and hobbled slowly along. They moved away from the crowds of people heading towards the main hotel building, to the bench he had pointed out earlier. It was set in front of a spectacular bed of red, full-blown roses, looking glorious in the June sunshine.

'Sit here,' he ordered.

Marina sank down onto the seat. She could still hear the bells pealing out.

'I love the sound of church bells,' Roberto remarked.

'Yes, but I'd want the real thing at my wedding,' she blurted.

'That's exactly what I think,' he smiled.

Marina looked around and breathed in the perfume of the flowers.

'Gorgeous, aren't they?' he said.

'Your dad certainly chose a good venue for his wedding. Or was it Amelia who selected it?'

'I've no idea. I know very little about the wedding preparations, and even less about Amelia,' Marina replied, tersely. 'But it is a lovely spot.'

Roberto looked at her.

'You don't sound very enthusiastic about your father's wedding,' he noted.

'Should I be?'

'I would have thought so.'

'Can we change the subject?' She didn't want to discuss her father.

'Okay. If that's what you want. Now, let me have a look at your ankle. I can tell you're in pain.'

'I'm sure it will be all right in a few minutes, when I've had a rest.'

'We'll see.'

Roberto gently lifted her ankle and examined it. After a few moments, he pronounced, 'I don't think you've done anything serious. You've just twisted it, which isn't surprising, considering the height of those heels. It'll probably be better in a few days, especially if you wear something more sensible. I don't suppose you have any flat shoes with you? It would be a lot easier for you to walk.'

'No, I haven't,' Marina burst out, indignantly. 'We're at a wedding, not out for a . . . a . . . hike. They match my outfit.'

'Maybe they do, but if you can't walk in them without having an accident, then they aren't much use to you.'

She knew what he said was true. She'd had her doubts about these shoes herself, but they were so pretty, she hadn't been able to resist buying them. It annoyed her, though, that he should say this. She sat up straight and glowered at him.

'Thank you very much for helping me, but it's really none of your concern.'

'Normally no, but it is when you practically fall at my feet.'

'I didn't fall! I just tripped up a bit.'

'And if I hadn't been close by, you

would have gone flat on your face, probably hurting yourself even more than you have already, and ruining your outfit. Not a good thing to happen at any time, but especially not at your father's wedding.'

'I'm sorry to have been such a bother to you,' Marina retorted, as haughtily as she could. 'I'll be okay when I've had a rest, so you can go now. Get back to your . . . parents and your . . . friends and . . . the . . . the reception,' she said, flapping her hands at him.

'You can't dismiss me that easily,' Roberto replied. 'I'm trying to help — although you don't seem to have the sense to realise it.'

'Maybe it's because of your pompous attitude.' Marina was beside herself with rage. She'd never met anyone so infuriating.

'Calm down! You're over-reacting. It's not good for your blood pressure, getting yourself in such a state.'

'And what would you know about that?'

'Quite a lot actually. I do have some medical training.'

So he was a doctor. Well, she didn't think much of his bedside manner! He was right though, she was over-reacting. She wasn't normally like this, but there was something about him that seemed to rub her up the wrong way.

'Are you going to let me help you?' Roberto looked at her with one eyebrow raised. 'Or shall I leave you here, in pain, to hobble back to the hotel by yourself?'

'I . . . I don't . . . '

'You need to hold onto someone,' he interrupted. 'Otherwise you'll go over again, and next time you might do yourself a greater injury. So what's it going to be? Make up your mind.'

Marina looked around. Most people had made their way to the main building. She could only see a few stragglers — young couples who were wrapped up in each other. They wouldn't notice her. She really had no choice but to do as he suggested.

'Okay, I give in. You can help me.' Marina's voice was subdued. She hated the thought of being dependent on him.

'You're so magnanimous!' he said sarcastically. 'Now, grab hold of my arm and I'll escort you to the hotel. You need some painkillers. I'll see if I can get you some water to go with them. I'm afraid alcohol wouldn't be a good idea, so I'd advise against you getting merry.'

'That was not my intention,' Marina said, between gritted teeth.

'Wasn't it? What's the matter, don't you want to celebrate your father's wedding?' He looked at her with narrowed eyes. 'You really don't seem keen on being here. Do you disapprove, or something?'

'I don't wish to discuss it.' Marina's teeth were still gritted in sheer frustration — the worst of it was, this arrogant know-it-all had hit the nail on the head.

'Fine. I'll keep quiet. Now, let's get going.'

Reluctantly, she took hold of Roberto's arm.

'Are you all right?' he asked, as they made their way slowly over to the main hotel building.

'Yes, thank you.' She was trying not to make a fuss. She wanted to get away from him as soon as possible. He made her feel inadequate and uncomfortable.

As they approached the hotel, he said, 'I expect your father's wondering where you are, Marina.'

'He probably is.' She glanced up at him enquiringly. 'How did you know my name?'

'My dad's mentioned it.'

'Your dad knows mine?'

'Yes. My parents are good friends of Amelia's parents, so I guess they've all met. Anyway, I heard my father say that Lionel has a daughter called Marina, and I remembered it; it's an unusual name. And I saw you standing next to your dad in all those endless photographs, and heard him talking to you.'

So she hadn't imagined it then — he

had been watching her!

'Does that explanation satisfy you?' Roberto was asking.

'I suppose Marina is a fairly uncommon name. I think there was someone in the royal family with it. Mum told me she'd always liked it, so that's how I came by it.'

'Very interesting.'

'And you're Roberto?'

'My mother's Italian.'

So that was the language they had been speaking. Marina still didn't know why Roberto was there though. Her curiosity overcame her, and she asked, 'How come you were invited to the wedding?'

'I . . . I'm a friend of Amelia.'

'Have you known her a long time then?'

'Most of my life. Now, have I answered all your questions? I didn't know I was in for an interrogation this afternoon.'

That was something of an exaggeration, Marina thought, but she kept quiet. She was feeling tired from walking in an awkward manner, trying to keep the weight off her strained ankle.

They had arrived back outside the hotel. They could hear a lot of noise coming from inside, people chatting and music blaring. A few guests were loitering around on the patio, drinking and enjoying the afternoon sunshine.

'Hold tight as we go up the steps. I don't want you having any more accidents.'

'I didn't have an accident. I just . . . tripped,' Marina argued, feeling foolish, as this was the very definition of an accident.

'My mistake — you fell and twisted your ankle on purpose, then?'

She tried to let go of Roberto's arm. She didn't want people — especially her father — to think she was with him. She wanted to get away. He was having a detrimental effect on her mood, and that hadn't been good to begin with.

'Now what are you doing?' Roberto

held onto her firmly. 'I told you to hold on tightly. These steps are steep and uneven. You could go crashing down.'

'I'm twenty-five, not ninety-five,' Marina protested. She looked around and was relieved to see that no one seemed to be taking any notice of them. 'Let go of me, please. I can manage.'

'On your head be it!' Roberto released her. 'If you trip again, don't expect me to rescue you.'

'I wouldn't dream of asking you,' she muttered in reply.

Roberto stepped back and let Marina go in front. She hobbled through the entrance to where Lionel and Amelia were standing, greeting all their guests.

'Marina! At last. And Roberto, isn't it?' Lionel exclaimed. 'I've been wondering where you were. I didn't know you two knew each other. Where have you been hiding? Or should I not be asking that question?' He smiled, knowingly. 'Most of the other guests have come in.'

Marina didn't smile. The last thing

she wanted was her father thinking she was getting up to something with this obnoxious man!

'We don't know each other,' she replied, quickly. 'We've only just met.'

'Hello, Marina,' Amelia interrupted. 'I've been meaning to tell you how lovely you look.'

'Thank you. So do you,' she mumbled, as Amelia hugged her. 'Your dress is beautiful.'

'I'm glad you like it. Oh, Marina, I'm so looking forward to spending time with you after the honeymoon, when everything's settled down; we can go shopping, have a meal together. What do you say?'

'Oh . . . That will be . . . fun.' She couldn't think of anything else to say. She had no intention of doing anything with Amelia, but could hardly say that.

'Pleased you've made it,' Lionel was saying, as he shook Roberto's hand. 'I know how busy you always are. Amelia's told me all about you.'

'Nothing bad, I hope?'

'No, she's given me a glowing report.'

Marina watched as Roberto took hold of Amelia's hand, kissed it and said, 'I hope you'll be very happy.'

He then turned to Lionel and said, 'Congratulations to you both. You're a lucky man.' Marina thought she could hear envy in his voice. Surely Roberto wasn't jealous of her father?

'I know. I'm very fortunate,' Lionel replied, kissing Amelia, before bending down to hug his daughter. 'I never thought I would be so happy again.'

Marina was aware that some other guests had entered the hotel behind them, so she started to move forward. It was then that Lionel noticed his daughter was hobbling.

'Marina, what have you done to yourself?'

Before she could reply, Roberto answered for her.

'Don't worry, Marina's okay. She just had a slight accident. I've been trying to help.' He looked at her. 'But I've got the feeling that it hasn't been appreciated.'

Lionel glanced at his daughter, who was keeping quiet.

'What happened?' he enquired, turning to Roberto. 'She didn't trip up by any chance, did she?'

'How did you guess?' Roberto grinned.

'I can answer for myself,' Marina fumed, glaring at both of them. 'I can speak.'

'Are you all right?' asked Amelia.

'I just twisted my ankle. It'll soon be better.'

'Has she done that before?' Roberto enquired, still grinning.

'It's not funny,' Marina grumbled. 'I don't know why you two look so amused.

'She will wear these high heels. I've told her so many times how dangerous they are,' Lionel answered.

'Don't tease her.' Amelia patted Marina's arm. 'I think your shoes are gorgeous. Some people have no idea about fashion. Take no notice of these two.'

'I won't.'

Roberto looked back at the guests waiting behind them.

'We'll see you two later. You have some more guests to greet. Come on, Marina, let's get you something to drink.'

He put his arm around her waist and led her over to a large table where the drinks were displayed. 'Now, what would you like?'

She couldn't seem get rid of him! But would it be so bad to be stuck with Roberto? Her thoughts were ambivalent. Part of her wanted to get away, but at the same time, she was strangely fascinated by this arrogant man. Also, she didn't relish the idea of being on her own for the rest of the festivities. All the other guests seemed to be with someone. She was beginning to regret declining her father's offer of bringing a friend.

'Sit here,' Roberto commanded, after she'd chosen her drink and selected a few nibbles. He rummaged in his jacket pocket. 'Take these painkillers now. They should start working in about half an hour.'

He stood looking down at her as she swallowed the capsules.

'You think of everything,' she murmured.

'I try to. Now, Marina, I don't want to monopolise you if you'd rather be elsewhere, but I guess, like me, you know hardly anyone here. Is that right?'

'How do you know that?'

'Well, I haven't noticed crowds of people coming up and speaking to you.'

'You've got me,' she admitted. 'Apart from my father and Amelia, I only recognise a few guests — mostly his work colleagues.'

'You have a small family?'

'I'm afraid so. No relatives that we ever see. After Mum died, it was just Dad and me, until . . . until Amelia came along.'

'You don't seem very pleased about that.'

'Are you?' The words were out before

she realised what she was saying.

'Why shouldn't I be?' Roberto stared at her.

'No reason. I don't know why I said that,' Marina replied quickly. If he was envious of her father for marrying Amelia, he certainly wouldn't tell her. 'I guess you probably know even fewer people than I do.'

'Yes; just Amelia, her parents, and mine. And I'm sure they won't want me tagging along with them all the time, so unless you have any objections, it looks as if we're stuck with each other.'

That was exactly what she'd been thinking.

'What do you say, Marina? Would you prefer to be on your own for the rest of the day?'

'No,' she admitted.

'Good.' Roberto said, sitting down beside her.

3

Marina took a sip of her drink, leaned back, and tried to make herself more comfortable.

'I guess we'll just have to make the best of it,' she said.

She hadn't anticipated being in this position, feeling obliged to make conversation with an exceedingly handsome, thoroughly arrogant man, who obviously didn't relish the idea of being left with her, either. She hadn't really given much thought to the actual wedding reception at all, to be honest; she'd been so caught up with being opposed to the marriage. Everything had been planned in such a hurry. If she'd had any sense, she wouldn't have rejected her father's offer of allowing her to bring a friend. At least then, she would have had someone of her own choice to talk to.

'You don't sound very sure about it,' Roberto was saying. 'If you want me to leave you alone, I will.'

'No, of course not. I'm sorry, I didn't mean to sound rude. I'd be glad of your company.'

'That's settled then. I won't have to wander around on my own, feeling like a fish out of water.'

Marina couldn't help smiling. She didn't think that was very likely. Roberto seemed the sort to be at ease wherever he was.

'Thank you for looking after me. I know I didn't sound very grateful before. I've no excuse.'

'You were in pain. That makes people short-tempered,' replied Roberto. 'I'm right, aren't I?'

'Yes. My ankle feels a lot better now, though. Thanks to you.'

'That's partly because you're resting it. I don't think you'll be able to do much dancing tonight, I'm afraid.'

'I think you might be right! And look, if you want to dance, please don't feel you have to stay with me all the time.'

'I can't leave you on your own. That wouldn't be very gentlemanly.'

'I wouldn't mind. Really, I wouldn't.'

'We'll see. Anyway, who would I dance with? Everyone seems to be in pairs.'

'That's true.'

'Would you like another drink?'

'Yes please, I'd love one.'

'You stay here and I'll be back in a flash.'

Marina watched Roberto as he strode over to the refreshment table. She was beginning to feel more relaxed. Maybe he was not as arrogant and self-assured as she had first thought.

She looked around at all the other guests. Roberto was right. They all seemed to be in pairs. Amongst them, she could see her dad and Amelia talking to a group of young people, whilst Roberto's father and mother were chatting to an elderly couple whom she presumed to be relatives or friends of Amelia's parents.

'I hope this is all right,' Roberto said, returning with two glasses. 'Fruit cocktail. Non-alcoholic, of course.'

'That's fine. Thanks. Do you have the same?'

'Yes, I have to drive back to London tonight.' He sat down next to her. 'I had a look at the seating plan for the meal while I was over there. You're next to your dad, and I'm at the other end of the table beside my mother, so you'll be able to escape from me for a while, at least, while we're eating,' Roberto smiled.

'More like the other way round — you get to escape from me,' Marina said, quickly.

'Not at all. I don't know why you would think that.'

'Sorry.'

'There you go again. You don't have to keep apologising.'

'I'll try not to.'

'Now, Marina, I think it's time we introduced ourselves properly. We didn't get off to a very good start.'

True enough, she thought.

'Okay. That's a good idea. You go first.'

'I'm Roberto Jefferson, I'm thirty-five, and I live and work in London. You?'

'Marina Scott, twenty-five, and I work for the same company as my father. I gather you're a doctor?'

'Oh no, nothing so grand.'

'I thought you said you had medical training?'

'Yes, I work as a paramedic. And when I'm off duty, I paint.'

'Do you mean pictures? Or you decorate houses?'

'Pictures.'

'That's interesting. I've never met an artist before.'

'I'd love to do it full-time, but it's not the greatest of earners unless you're well known.'

'It's certainly an unusual combination.'

'I suppose it is. My father's a doctor, and he wanted me to follow in his footsteps.'

'Fathers often do! Mine helped me get my job. Go on.'

'Well, right from when I was very young, I had the urge to paint. I went to Art College — much to the annoyance of my dad — but when I left, I couldn't find a suitable job. I didn't want to teach and, obviously, growing up, I was aware of my father's work, so I'd always had an interest in medicine too. I decided to train as a paramedic. Which made Dad a bit happier! I work long shifts, but I also get days off, so I can spend time doing my painting too.'

'I should think it's hard, being a paramedic. You must see some terrible things.'

'It can be upsetting. But when you know you've made a difference to someone's life, it's incredibly rewarding.'

'I'm sure it must be. What about your pictures? Have you sold any?'

'Quite a few, actually, and I've exhibited at some local shows in London.'

'That's great! What medium do you use?'

'Acrylics and water colours.'

'I'd love to see some of your pictures.' As soon as the words left her lips, Marina regretted them. After today, she'd probably never see him again. He'd be miles away, in London.

'Would you really?' Roberto looked surprised. 'Well, anyway, I think that's enough about me. Tell me more about yourself. What do you do in your spare time?'

'Nothing as interesting as you. Just the normal stuff, really. Reading, going to the theatre, eating out, listening to music.'

'What's wrong with that?'

'Nothing, I suppose. They're not creative activities, though. I don't actually produce anything. I can't play an instrument. I'm not even very good at cooking.'

'You're probably being too modest. Anyway, does it matter? Not everyone's the same. The important thing is you enjoy what you do.'

'Oh, I do. I've an enormous collection of books and music.'

'I'd like to . . . '

'Hello there!' Lionel interrupted whatever Roberto had been about to say. Marina looked up, startled. She'd been so engrossed in her conversation with Roberto that she hadn't seen her father approaching. He and Amelia had been circulating amongst their guests and had arrived in front of them, their arms entwined.

'These two look very cosy,' he joked to Amelia.

'Don't they just?' she answered, without smiling. 'I'm beginning to get a bit tired from all this parading around. I think it's time we had a rest.' She sank down onto a spare seat, close to Roberto.

Lionel kissed her on the cheek. 'I'm sorry darling. You should have told me.'

'It's these shoes,' she stage-whispered to her new husband. 'They're killing me.'

He grinned. 'Now, where have I heard that before?'

Roberto laughed, and even Marina had to smile.

'Are you enjoying yourselves?' Lionel asked them. 'I noticed you were engaged in earnest conversation. That's why we didn't disturb you before.'

'I am, thanks,' Roberto answered.

'And you?' Lionel looked at his daughter.

'Yes, thank you.'

'Neither of us knows many people here,' Roberto continued, 'and Marina can't move around too much because of her ankle, so I'm keeping her company.'

'That's very good of you. She only knows a few guests. I was hoping she'd find someone she got along with. Where have your parents got to, Roberto?'

'I've no idea. I haven't seen them for quite a while.'

'Chatting to mine, I expect,' Amelia answered. 'You know what they're like, Roberto. When they get together, they never stop talking. I don't know who's the worst, my mum or yours.'

'It's her Italian blood. She gets a bit excited,' Roberto said, smiling at Amelia.

'Yes, do you remember when my parents came back from Italy and had seen the Pope? Your mother wanted to know every little detail about it!'

'How could I forget? She talked of nothing else for days. I'd just moved into my flat, and she kept ringing me up, telling me all about it.'

'Yes! And . . . '

'Very interesting,' Lionel remarked, interrupting Amelia. 'You'll have to tell me about it another time.'

Marina had felt left out of the conversation, and guessed her dad had too, with Roberto and Amelia discussing past events that only involved them. There was no one there she could reminisce with — apart from her dad, of course, but he was too besotted with Amelia to be bothered with her now. Besides, he had several friends here from years back; Marina had no one.

Lionel was looking down. 'How's your foot, Marina?'

'It's much better, thank you.'

'Good.' He turned to Amelia. 'It'll be time for the wedding breakfast soon, so I think we'd better go and find our places.' He helped her up from the seat and then said to his daughter, 'You'll be next to me, Marina. I'm sorry you and Roberto will be split up.'

'You don't have to be sorry,' she replied. 'We're grown-ups. I'm sure we can handle it.'

'She's looking forward to escaping from me,' Roberto added, and Lionel laughed as he and Amelia moved away.

They sat, people-watching, until they heard the announcement that their meal was ready to be served. Roberto escorted Marina to her place, and then strode to the opposite end of the room, where he was seated next to his mother. She watched him go, thinking he was the most attractive man she'd ever met, but the most difficult to understand.

Marina sat through the meal, chatting to some of the other guests who were close by. She occasionally exchanged a word with her father, but most of the time he only had eyes for Amelia, who said very little to Marina.

She thought back to earlier on that day, when she'd practically fallen into Roberto's arms. After the wedding, she doubted she would ever see him again, which saddened her. She found him fascinating, yet at the same time, irritating. She also couldn't help speculating about him and Amelia. From the way they had acted around each other, Marina had a feeling that, at some point, they had been more than just friends. Was her father aware of this, she wondered?

Finally, after several speeches, the meal came to an end and everyone adjourned to the lounge, where seats had been placed around the perimeter, leaving a large, empty space in the centre.

Marina hobbled to an armchair and

sank down onto it. Her ankle was beginning to hurt again. A few minutes later, Roberto and his parents appeared beside her.

'Hello. How is your foot?' his mother asked, in a strong Italian accent, patting her on the shoulder. 'I was most worried.'

'It's not too bad, thank you for asking,' Marina replied.

'I hope my son looked after you?'

'Yes, he's been very kind,' she said, smiling at him.

Roberto looked awkward at her praise, then said, 'I'm forgetting my manners — please, let me introduce you all properly.'

For the next few minutes, Roberto's father, William, and his mother, Sophia, sat chatting to Marina. She thought them both charming, and amused herself wondering why their son didn't possess their social graces.

'So pleased to have met you, Marina,' William said, eventually. 'I hope we'll have that pleasure again soon. Come along, Sophia, let's leave the young people on their own. I'm sure they don't want to spend much time with us old folks.'

After they had walked away, Marina remarked, 'What a lovely couple your parents are!'

'You think so?'

'Yes. Don't sound so shocked.'

'Well, I suppose I see a different side to them.'

'Because of your father's opposition to your career?'

'I guess that's it. We'll never see eye to eye about that. Anyway, did you enjoy the meal?' Roberto asked.

'Yes, thank you. It was very good.'

'I thought so, too.'

The small band started to play, and Lionel and Amelia stepped into the centre of the room for the first dance, which was a waltz. Gradually, other couples joined them.

'Would you like to dance, or is your ankle too painful?' Roberto asked.

'I'll have a go,' Marina replied.

Soon they were gliding around the floor. She was enjoying being held in Roberto's arms, despite the nagging pain in her ankle. He said very little, and seemed to be concentrating on the music. When the waltz finished, he led her over to an armchair.

'I think that's enough for now. You'd better rest.'

'Okay.'

Roberto did an exaggerated double-take. 'You agreed with what I said — you *must* be in pain!' he exclaimed.

'I don't disagree with everything,' Marina answered. 'But you're right, my ankle does hurt.'

'I'll get you a drink and some more painkillers. I won't be long.'

Am I really so disagreeable? Marina wondered. She didn't think she was, usually — but there was something about Roberto that seemed to make her act quite out of character.

When he returned and they'd finished their drinks, she said, 'There's no need to stay with me all the time, you

57

can go and dance with someone else if you like. I'm quite happy to sit here and watch.'

'That's kind of you.'

Again, Marina wasn't sure if he meant it, or was being sarcastic.

'Who should I dance with?' Roberto continued. 'I know so few people. Besides, everyone's already paired up.'

Marina noticed that Amelia was sitting down, alone, at the opposite end of the room. 'What about Amelia?'

'She'll be with Lionel, of course.'

'She's on her own, look. I don't know where Dad is. Why don't you go and ask her?'

'If you insist.'

'I do.'

Marina looked on as he strode across the room and stood facing Amelia. He didn't take a lot of persuading to do that, she thought. Amelia got up and followed him onto the dance floor. The music started up for a tango. Marina was glad she was sitting out. She had never mastered the steps for that dance.

She watched, entranced, as Roberto and Amelia spun round, both brilliant dancers. They seemed to be deep in conversation as they moved in perfect unison. Marina wondered what they were talking about. When she'd waltzed with Roberto, he had been silent.

'All on your own?' She looked up to see Lionel standing in front of her.

'I'm resting my ankle. Why aren't you dancing?'

'I'm no good at the tango. Too old for that now, but I'm glad Amelia's found someone to partner her.'

'You don't mind, then?'

'No, why should I? She's younger than me. I don't want to restrict her because of my age.'

'I see.'

'I don't know if you do. I have the feeling that you don't like Amelia.'

'I haven't said that.'

'You don't have to. I can tell by the way you look when you see her. I know you think she's too young for me, and you aren't happy about me getting married again, but I hope you'll get over that. Anyway, you've got yourself a nice young man to keep you occupied.'

'Who?' Marina stared at him, a puzzled look on her face.

'Roberto, of course. Is there someone else, then?'

'No, but I'm not with Roberto. I only met him today.'

'I realise that, but you seem to be getting on well together. I have a feeling you rather like him. Is that right? He seems a nice enough chap. I gather he's known Amelia since they were children.'

'I really know very little about him.'

'You're so touchy, Marina. Right, I think I'd better go and reclaim my bride.' Lionel moved away, and stood waiting until the dance ended, then went up to Roberto and Amelia, leading his new wife away.

Marina felt uncomfortable — now her dad was complaining about her! She really must be as difficult as

Roberto had said. She determined to try and be more amenable to everyone.

Roberto wandered over to Marina, having got himself another drink.

'I'm glad you were having a chat with your dad. I felt a bit bad about leaving you on your own.'

'I really didn't mind. You don't have to feel chained to me. Did you actually enjoy the tango?'

'Yes. Why shouldn't I?' he asked.

'I just think it's quite hard. I'm no good at it, but you and Amelia were brilliant.'

'You just need some practice, I expect,' he replied, sidestepping the compliment.

★　★　★

The rest of the evening passed uneventfully. Marina tried hard to curb her tongue and there were no further altercations with Roberto. He danced a few more times with Amelia, while Marina chatted to some of her father's friends. She was still in two minds about Roberto, not being fully at ease with him, yet not wanting the evening to end.

All too soon, though, it was time for the final waltz. Roberto asked Marina to dance with him and, again, they danced in silence. His face was inscrutable and she had no idea what was going through his mind.

Everyone gathered around afterwards to wave Lionel and Amelia off on their honeymoon, to some unknown destination — Lionel had booked it himself, a surprise for his new wife.

'Let me know when you've arrived safely, and where you are,' Marina urged.

'I will,' he promised. 'And you take care too. No more accidents! Get yourself some sensible shoes.'

'Don't listen to him,' Amelia called.

Marina smiled and waved as they drove off. It was clear that Amelia wanted to be friends, and, for the first time, it occurred to Marina that Amelia may be finding it all quite difficult too, marrying a man who had a daughter only ten years younger than herself. Amelia was her step-mother now — what a strange thought!

The wedding guests were beginning to drift away. Marina turned to Roberto to say that she would collect her things and go home.

'I think I'd better be on my way too. I'm working tomorrow,' he replied. 'Did you come by car? Or do you need a lift anywhere?'

'No, I'm okay. I drove here. Thank you for asking though, and for looking after me,' she answered.

'Will you be able to manage with your bad ankle?'

'Yes. I'll be fine. It's only a ten minute drive back home. It was nice meeting you.'

'The pleasure was all mine. Marina . . . ' He hesitated, before continuing, haltingly, 'would you . . . perhaps be interested in . . . us . . . having a meal together some time?'

This was so unexpected, she was lost for words.

'Oh . . . I . . . I . . . '

'It's all right,' Roberto interrupted. 'I shouldn't have asked.'

'No. I'm glad you did. I would like that very much.' It was true, she thought.

'You would? Really?'

'Yes, please.'

'Good,' he smiled.

He escorted Marina to her car and they exchanged telephone numbers. As she got in, he called, 'I'll be in touch in a few days. Goodnight Marina. Drive carefully.'

He stood watching as she drove away.

4

That night in bed, Marina reflected on the day. She felt pleased that it had gone well for her father, and hoped that he and his new wife would be happy together. She vowed that she would put her misgivings behind her, and try to get on with Amelia. After all, her dad was married now. There was nothing she could do about it, so she would have to make the best of it.

The dominant thoughts, though, concerned Roberto. Her father's wedding was the last place she would have expected to meet someone. Roberto was the most attractive man she had ever met, but she definitely found him disturbing. He wasn't like any other man she had known. They were usually more straightforward. You knew where you were with them. Roberto however, was much more complex. He was arrogant and sarcastic one moment, and then suddenly, he seemed to be vulnerable and lacking in confidence. She'd been infuriated by him, yet had found him irresistible.

These were new feelings for Marina, and she didn't know how to deal with them. She'd wanted him to ask her out, but when he had, she'd been so surprised she hadn't known what to say. He'd told her he would ring and arrange a date. Would he really, she wondered, or would he change his mind when he got home? She hoped not, but knew she'd be very nervous if he did contact her again.

Marina thought back to her previous boyfriend. Oh, why had Jon had to go and move to Australia? Life had been much less complicated when they were together. Had she made a mistake in not going with him? Now her dad was married, she'd see a lot less of him, so her main reason for not having gone — that she couldn't leave her father — no longer applied. She and Jon had got on well together, Marina mused, and she'd felt comfortable in his presence. There'd been no great passion, but that had suited her. She thought maybe she just wasn't a very passionate person.

All these thoughts drifted round in her head until, finally, she fell into a restless sleep, waking late the next morning. Marina was glad it was Sunday and she didn't have to go to work.

She stepped out of bed gingerly, and flinched when her foot touched the floor. She looked down and noticed that her ankle was slightly swollen. She decided to go to the chemist and buy a bandage for it. That should help her get to and from work the next day. Luckily, she lived close to a parade of shops, so she hobbled slowly along, made her purchase and returned to her flat.

Marina spent the rest of the day catching up on her household chores, which fortunately didn't take too long, and then she relaxed on the balcony, soaking up the sun and reading a paperback. Why was it, she pondered, that in novels, no matter how many problems there were, the ending was nearly always happy, whereas in real life it often wasn't? She guessed that readers wanted to escape from their troubles and indulge in a happy, fantasy world for a brief time. She wondered if there would be a happy outcome for her. And for her dad and Amelia.

Marina jumped as her mobile phone played its jaunty little tune. She picked it up and was startled to see Roberto's number on the screen. She hadn't expected him to call so soon.

'Hello, Marina. How's your ankle?'

'Not too bad, thank you. How are you?' She could feel her heart thumping madly. That didn't happen when Jon used to ring her, she reflected.

'I'm fine. What have you been doing today?'

'Catching up on my housework and sitting on my balcony. You?'

'Similar to you, except that I

attended Mass this morning with my mother. Then I tidied up my flat and did some washing, but I haven't got a balcony to sit on, unfortunately.'

'I'd hate it if I didn't have some open space. I like the fresh air,' Marina replied.

'So do I, but in London it's not so fresh.'

'I guess not. Do your parents live near you, then?'

'Not far away.'

'Do you see a lot of them?'

'Once a week usually, but it was Mum's birthday. I had to take her a present and she asked me to go to Mass with her. Then she was going out for lunch with my dad.'

'You didn't want to eat with them?'

'Oh no, they wanted a romantic lunch together,' Roberto laughed. 'They didn't want me tagging along. They can be like a couple of love birds when they're alone together. Have you heard from your father? Do you know where they've gone for their honeymoon?'

'Not yet, no. I think they have other things on their mind rather than ringing me. My dad will probably text later.'

'Do you think you'll manage at work tomorrow with your bad ankle?'

'I'm sure I will. It's only slightly swollen today.'

'Good. I hope it will soon feel better. Now, shall we make a date for next Saturday? You should be recovered by then, I hope.'

'That would be nice,' Marina replied, with butterflies in her stomach. 'You won't be working then?'

'No. I'm doing one extra shift this week, but I'll be off duty from Friday until Sunday. So if we go out on Saturday, I'll have Friday and Sunday to work on my pictures. I'm copying some photographs I've taken at the moment, mostly scenic views.'

'Is that your speciality?'

'I enjoy doing that, but I do other things as well: animals, buildings. Not people, though. I'm not so good on them. Is there anywhere in particular you'd like to go out?'

'I don't mind where we go. Shall I drive over to meet you somewhere?'

'No, let me come to you.'

'Are you sure? It's a long way for you to drive over here from London.'

'I don't think so. It wasn't too far yesterday. And wasn't the reception venue fairly close to where you live?'

'Yes, it is.'

'Where are you exactly?'

'Mallory Wood.'

'Yes, I've heard of it. I think I may have passed through, actually, but I've never stopped there. It won't take long to drive to you, and I'll be interested to see the place. Shall we have dinner out? Do you know of any good restaurants?'

'Yes, several.'

'As you know the area and I don't, would you mind choosing one and booking a table for us?'

'Of course not.'

'Right. Book it for eight o'clock on Saturday evening. I'll look up Mallory Wood on my sat nav. I'll try to arrive a bit earlier, say seven o'clock, so you can show me around. What's your exact address?'

After telling Roberto how to find her flat, he ended the conversation by saying, 'Have a good week Marina. See you Saturday.'

That was a pleasant surprise, she thought as she put the phone down, her fingers trembling. He hadn't wasted much time in contacting her again. She really hadn't been sure he would. It occurred to her they'd both been chatting quite easily to each other, without any of the awkwardness there had been at her father's wedding. Now she had something to look forward to, and it was all thanks to her dad. If he hadn't married Amelia, she would never have met Roberto.

★ ★ ★

Later that day, Marina had a phone call from Lionel.

'We're in Jersey,' he told her.

'Everything's wonderful. I hope you enjoyed yesterday.'

'Yes, I did.' Marina realised she was telling the truth. After being a reluctant guest, everything had turned out better than she could have imagined. Of course, she was seeing things somewhat differently now. Everything was coloured by the fact that Roberto had arranged to go out with her on Saturday. If he hadn't got in touch again, she might not have seen things so rosily.

'How's your ankle?' Lionel enquired.

'Getting better, thanks, and thank you for ringing. Have a lovely honeymoon, Dad. I'll see you when you get back.'

Marina was very busy at work for the next few days. She received several enquiries from her workmates about her father's wedding, and her friend, Lisa, rang on Wednesday evening, also wanting to know all the details about Saturday. Just as she had done at work, Marina enthused about the event. Lisa sounded surprised.

'You have changed your tune,' she said. 'You weren't looking forward to it at all last week!'

'Well, I suppose I was wrong to be opposed to it. It's my dad's life after all. I should be more supportive.'

'What's brought on this change of heart?'

'Nothing, really,' said Marina, innocently.

'There's something suspicious here,' said Lisa. 'Who did you go to the wedding with?'

'No one.'

'In that case, who did you leave it with?'

'Lisa! No one!'

'Well, all I know is, last week you were bemoaning the fact that your dad was getting married to someone he hardly knew, and now, you're singing praises about it. Something must have happened to change your mind!'

'The wedding went well, that's all I'm saying.'

'Okay, okay! I'm glad it was a success.'

Lisa clearly knew her too well! But the last thing Marina wanted to do was tell her about Roberto. It was early days yet. She wanted to wait and see how things went before she mentioned him to anyone.

Finally, Saturday arrived. Marina spent a lot of time getting ready for the occasion. She was excited, but at the same time, nervous. Suppose they didn't get on? She'd booked a table at a restaurant in Mallory Wood that she liked, and had decided would be a good place for their first date. Would there be others, Marina wondered?

At seven o'clock, Roberto rang her doorbell.

'You look very nice,' he said, when she opened the door. Marina thought he looked even more handsome than she remembered, but she didn't say anything.

'As it's a lovely evening, I thought you might like to show me around

Mallory Wood before we eat?' he suggested. 'That is, if your ankle's better.'

'Yes, much better, thank you. We can have a little walk, and then head to the restaurant — it's not too far away. That's what I like about this town. It's quite compact. Everything is within walking distance from my flat. Come inside a minute while I get a jacket for later.'

Roberto followed Marina into the lounge, looking around admiringly as he did so.

'You have a beautiful flat,' he said. 'And it's so tidy.'

'It wasn't this morning. I had to do some housework earlier.'

'That's what mine needs, but I've been too busy getting on with my painting. I can't seem to keep it tidy. I'll try to have a go at it when I'm off duty next.'

'Well, you've got an excuse. Your art materials must take up a lot of space.'

'They do.' He glanced around the

room. 'Wow. You have a large collection of CDs.'

'Yes, bit of a throwback, but I'm reluctant to get rid of them. I started collecting them when I was at school.'

He walked over and studied the shelves. 'I've got quite a few of these. We must have had similar tastes in music growing up.' Roberto turned to smile at Marina, and then said, 'Ready?'

Five minutes later, they were strolling along a gravel path beside the river, where countless ducks, geese and other birds were swimming about, enjoying the evening sunshine.

'This is very picturesque,' Roberto remarked.

'Yes. I love it. I often come and sit here, just watching the river. I look at those birds, flying about as countless generations of them have done before, and all my worries seem to melt away.' Now, why had she told him that? Roberto would be wondering what problems she had. True, she'd come here a lot when she'd been debating whether to go to Australia with Jon, but she really didn't want to discuss that with Roberto.

'Have you got a lot of worries then?'

'Not really. What about you?' Marina quickly deflected the conversation away from herself.

'Just about my painting, and photography; if my pictures will be good enough for the exhibition; if I can eventually make a living from it.'

'So, you'd give up your paramedic work?'

'Yes, I think I would. Although it's useful to have that as a fall-back. I enjoy my job — but I love my painting.'

'I didn't realise you did photography as well. You could have taken the photographs for Dad's wedding!'

'I wasn't asked,' he said, abruptly, and Marina sensed he wanted to change the subject.

'Could you paint this scene, do you think?' She stopped and gazed at the river.

'Yes.' Roberto stood beside her. 'It's

beautiful. I'd have to take some photos first, go away and study them.'

'Could you sit here and paint it?'

'If I was here long enough.'

'Have you got your camera with you?'

'I have. I always carry it.'

'Why don't you take some photos then?

'I didn't think that was very appropriate on a first date. I thought you might be annoyed,' he grinned.

Marina laughed. 'Of course I wouldn't be annoyed. You take some photos, Roberto, and I'll look forward to seeing them eventually, as well as your painting.'

As soon as she'd said that, Marina regretted it. Would he think she was being a bit presumptuous? After all, she didn't know what was going to happen in the future. This might be their only date.

'Okay,' Roberto smiled, 'but it might take a while.'

'We have time.'

An hour later, they were seated in a smart restaurant, beside a window that overlooked the town square, with its seasonal flower beds and seventeenth-century church.

'I had no idea Mallory Wood was such an attractive place,' Roberto remarked. 'How did it get its name?'

'Before the town developed, it was mostly woodland. There were just a few large estates. It's said that Henry the Eighth came here for a holiday to stay with his wealthy friend, Lord Arthur Mallory, who owned one of the grand houses. Henry liked the area so much, that he persuaded some of his other friends to move here. Gradually, the town developed, and Henry christened it Mallory Wood. If you walk to the end of the high street, you still come to a wooded area.'

'You know a lot about the place. Have you always lived here?' Roberto asked.

'All my life. I was born in the local hospital. I went to school here, and now, I live pretty close to the advertising agency where I work. Dad's one of the directors there.'

'Tell me more about your father. I'm curious about him.'

'Well, when he left university, he started as the office junior in the company, and gradually worked his way up to becoming a director. He bought the house he's living in now, just before I was born; he and Amelia are planning to move away, though, further out into the country. Mallory Wood is not rural enough for her, but you probably knew that already.'

'No, I didn't know that.'

'Did Amelia live near you in London?'

'Yes; her parents' house was not far from ours.'

'So she lived right in the city, then?'

'That's right.'

'What about when she grew up?'

'Still in London; she got her own flat.

What's all this fascination with Amelia?'

'I just don't know much about her. It was such a whirlwind romance. All I know is that my dad met her on a singles holiday.'

'Yes, that's what I heard. So, what are you going to have to eat? The menu looks fantastic.'

It seemed Roberto wanted to change the subject. She wondered why he was so reluctant to talk about her. It did seem to fit with her earlier notion that there had been something between them.

The waiter arrived with their drinks and took their order, and shortly after, they tucked into their starters. Although Marina had been nervous at first, she was now enjoying herself and conversation flowed freely; Amelia wasn't mentioned again.

When they had finished their meal, Roberto escorted Marina back to her flat.

'I've really enjoyed this evening. I hope you did too,' he said, as they stood outside her front door.

'Yes, I did. Very much. Thank you.'

'Good. So — might you fancy coming up to London next Saturday? We could go to one of the parks, or to a matinee if the weather is bad. What do you say?'

'I'd love to.'

'You would?'

'Yes Roberto, I would. Don't look so surprised!'

'In that case, I'll see you then. Goodnight, Marina.' Roberto leaned forward and gently kissed her on both cheeks. Then he turned and walked away.

5

Marina lay in bed that night feeling more happy and contented than she had for a long time. Her date with Roberto had gone very well — much better than she'd expected — and she was looking forward to their next meeting. She felt that the barrier which existed between them was diminishing. Maybe there had never been a barrier she mused; perhaps it had all been in her imagination. She wondered what Roberto thought about their blossoming relationship. Did he also feel that everything was going well, after that shaky start they had at her father's wedding?

Two days later she received a telephone call from her father.

'Marina, my dear, I'm just ringing to let you know we are back.'

'Hello Dad, how are you? How was

your honeymoon?'

'Wonderful. I haven't been so happy for years. Not since . . . '

'That's good, Dad,' Marina interrupted, just glad to hear that her dad was happy. And so was she! 'I'm glad you had a lovely time. How's Amelia?'

'She's fine, looks more beautiful than ever, but then, I suppose I am biased. I'm just amazed that such an attractive, young woman should want to get involved with an old boy like me.'

'You're not old, Dad. Amelia's the lucky one, to have you.'

'If you say so, dear. Thanks. Anyway, what have you been up to while I've been away?'

'Well, we've been very busy at the office, as I am sure you've guessed. Everyone asked after you, so I told them all about the big day. They'll be glad to see you back.'

'I've a few more days off yet before I have to go back, and so has Amelia.'

'What are you planning to do with them?'

'Just relaxing mainly, but we might make a few excursions; go down to the coast possibly, and have some meals out.'

'That'll be nice.'

'What else have you been doing besides working hard? Anything interesting?'

Marina hesitated. Should she tell her father about her date with Roberto?

But before she could reply, he suggested, 'Why don't you come round tomorrow evening? We can have a good old chat then.'

'I'd like that, although it won't be very early. We're working late in my department, and someone's ordering in pizzas for us, so I won't want anything to eat.'

'Okay, we'll just have drinks then. I'll ring off now Marina, I'm a bit tired after the flight. I know it's only a short one, but all that waiting around at the airport wears me out.'

Or is it Amelia that's wearing him out, Marina thought? Out loud, she said, 'Yes, it is tiring at airports. Goodnight, Dad. See you tomorrow.'

She had just hung up when her mobile phone sounded. She was delighted to see Roberto's number.

'Hello, Marina, how are you and how's your ankle?'

'I'm fine, and my ankle is too.'

'Very pleased to hear that.'

'I've just been speaking to Dad.'

'Are they back from their honeymoon already?'

'Yes, they got home today.'

'That was quick! If I ever get to have a honeymoon, I'll make it last as long as I can. I'm surprised Amelia didn't suggest they stay away longer.'

'Dad seemed very happy about everything.'

'That's good. I wonder if Amelia was.'

What was it with this guy and Amelia? Either he clammed up when her name was mentioned, or he couldn't stop talking about her.

She ignored Roberto's remark, and

replied, 'Did you get much painting done on Sunday after all?'

'Yes. I started on a new one.'

'What are you painting?' she asked.

'You'll have to wait and see,' he replied, laughing.

'Now, you've got me intrigued. What is it?'

'I'm not saying. I'll show you when it's finished. Then you can let me know what you think about it. Right, I'd better go. I'll see you on Saturday, Marina.'

'Okay. Bye.'

She put the phone down feeling quite elated.

★   ★   ★

The next evening, Marina went straight from work to her father's house. Amelia opened the door, kissed her on the cheek and said, 'It's lovely to see you.'

'You look well,' Marina remarked, noting Amelia's golden tan.

'We had sunshine every day. It was

perfect, not too hot, not too cold. I wish we could have stayed longer, but Lionel insisted we had a few days at home before he had to go back to work.'

Roberto had been right, Marina thought. Amelia had wanted a longer honeymoon.

'I'm glad you enjoyed it,' she replied.

'Go into the lounge,' Amelia urged. 'Lionel's just watching the cricket. Sports mad, that man!'

Marina found her father staring at the screen.

'Just getting the cricket scores,' he said, beaming at his daughter. 'I'll be with you in a minute.'

'That's okay. I'm used to it.' Marina remembered all the times when she'd been at home with her parents, and her father had been glued to the television set, watching the test match. Her mother used to mock-complain about being a cricket widow.

'Would you like a drink?' Amelia asked.

'I'd love a coffee, please.'

'Me too,' Lionel called, as his wife turned to leave the room.

He switched off the television, came over to Marina, and gave her a big hug.

'You weren't too late, then.'

'No. I worked really hard and managed to get everything done quickly.'

'It's good to be back,' Lionel murmured. 'We had a wonderful time, but it's always nice to come home, especially to this house. It has such good memories. I'll miss it when we move.'

'They're not all good memories, Dad.'

'You're right, but somehow, this house feels part of me. Do you understand what I mean?'

'Yes, I think I do. You've lived here so long, you can't imagine living anywhere else. I still think of this house as my home, even though I've not lived in it for a few years, now. I suppose it's because I grew up here. I'll miss it too, when you go. It won't be the same, visiting you in a different place.'

'No; it's going to be a real wrench leaving. I've lived here most of my adult life.'

'Have you told Amelia how you feel?'

'Yes, but I don't think she understands.'

'What don't I understand?' Amelia had returned with the drinks.

'We were just discussing moving, and I was saying how much I will miss this house.'

'Oh, it's nice enough, but you'll soon get used to somewhere else. It's only bricks and mortar, after all.'

'It's a bit more than that,' said Marina, springing to her father's defence.

'That's enough talk about moving,' Lionel cut in. 'I was going to tell you about our honeymoon.'

'Don't bore the poor girl,' Amelia countered. 'I'm sure she won't be interested.'

'I am, actually,' Marina answered. 'Go on, Dad, tell me about it.'

They sat drinking their coffee, while Lionel went into great detail about the hotel where they had stayed, the excursions they had made, and how marvellous it all was, while Amelia sat quietly, drinking. Marina thought that, if anything, *she* was the one who looked bored.

'You did a lot in a short time,' Marina remarked.

'We certainly did.' Suddenly, unexpectedly, Lionel asked, 'Have you heard any more from Roberto, by the way?'

'Oh . . . As a matter of fact, yes,' Marina stammered.

'You have? Good. I wondered if you would. What did he say?'

'He asked me to go out with him, actually.'

'And did you?'

'Yes.'

Marina thought that Amelia was looking more alert now, or was she just imagining it?

'I am glad. How did it go, and are you going to see him again?'

'What is this, the Spanish Inquisition?' Marina asked her father.

'No, of course not,' Lionel smiled. 'I'm just curious, that's all. You and Roberto seemed to be getting on so well at our wedding. You looked right together, somehow, so I had hoped . . . '

Marina interrupted. 'Dad, we were thrust together at the wedding due to circumstances, so don't read too much into it.'

'Okay, okay. Not another word from me on the matter,' said her father, before immediately continuing, 'But he's such a good-looking young man . . . '

'Good looks aren't everything,' Amelia muttered.

Lionel and Marina both looked at her in surprise.

'I suppose not,' he conceded. 'But Roberto seems to be a very pleasant fellow.'

'You hardly know him,' Amelia retorted.

'We might not know him, but you've known him practically all your life,' said

Lionel, looking quizzical. 'So come on, what dark secret is Roberto hiding? What do you know about him that we don't?'

'Nothing,' Amelia mumbled. 'I was just pointing out that you can't judge a person on looks or first impressions.'

'Well,' Lionel said, 'It seems you'd better watch out, Marina. Be careful how you go with Roberto.'

There was a brief, awkward silence, before conversation on other topics commenced.

What had all that been about, Marina wondered? Clearly, something must have happened between Roberto and Amelia in the past. It felt as if Amelia resented her getting involved with Roberto, but she couldn't understand why. After all, Amelia was married to Lionel now.

She was very aware of Amelia's gaze, which felt none too friendly. She spent the rest of the evening chatting with her father; Roberto wasn't mentioned again, and although Amelia joined in on occasions, Marina felt the animosity between them.

★   ★   ★

Marina was late home from work again the next day. She felt exhausted. She hurried in, kicked off her shoes, sank down onto the sofa, curled up and closed her eyes, feeling too tired to even think about preparing a meal for herself. Almost immediately, she fell into a deep sleep.

Sometime later, her dreams were interrupted by a persistent ringing sound. She opened her eyes, realising it was her home phone. Groggily she got up, grabbed the receiver and murmured, 'Hello?'

'Marina, thank goodness. I was beginning to think you weren't in.'

She didn't recognise the voice. 'Sorry, who is this?'

'It's Jon's mother,' the woman said impatiently, as if Marina should have known at once who it was. Why would

Jon's mother be ringing her? She hardly knew the woman.

'Oh . . . Hello, Mrs. Bentley.'

'I know you must be surprised to hear from me, and I don't want to upset you but . . . ' Her voice faltered. 'It's Jon. He's been in an accident.'

Marina's heart missed a beat.

'Oh no. Is he hurt?'

'Yes, it's quite serious, I'm afraid.' Mrs Bentley choked back a sob.

It must be bad if his mother was ringing her. She guessed that Mrs Bentley felt obliged to let her know, in case . . . Marina shuddered. It was too terrible to contemplate.

She wanted to know the details of the accident but thought it best not to ask. The woman sounded so distraught; she didn't want to upset her more.

Instead, she said, 'I hope he soon recovers. Please, let me know how he gets on.'

'We need your help, Marina.'

'My help? What help can I give? Jon's in Australia, isn't he?'

'The thing is,' Mrs Bentley continued, ignoring Marina's question, 'Jon was unconscious for a couple of days, but now he's come round, he keeps asking for you. He wants to see you, Marina.'

6

'To see me?' Marina mumbled, incredulously.

'Yes. He keeps calling your name.'

'But he hasn't seen me for ages. Why would he want to do that? Anyway, how can I see him? He's in Australia.'

'No. He's not in Australia, he's in Scotland.'

'Scotland? I don't understand.' Marina was feeling confused. She couldn't follow this conversation.

'Let me explain.' Mrs Bentley cleared her throat. 'I'm calling you from Edinburgh.'

'So, Jon's left Australia?'

'Not for good. He still has a job there, but he came home for a holiday. He'd decided to go to Scotland for a few days before . . . ' Mrs Bentley choked back a sob. 'Before coming to stay with me. He'd always wanted to go there.'

'So he was in Scotland when he had the accident?' Marina asked.

'Yes, on a coach. It crashed. He was going on a guided tour of Edinburgh when it happened. A speeding car came heading towards them without warning, and . . . ' Mrs Bentley burst into tears, 'and . . . it crashed into the front of the coach.'

'Oh, I'm so sorry.' She remembered hearing on the news there'd been a coach crash a few days previously, but she hadn't really taken it in.

'The driver braked hard and swerved away, but there was nothing else he could do to avoid the car. It clipped the front of the coach and turned over. Luckily, no other vehicles were involved. The police were full of praise for the coach driver. Said he'd probably saved the passengers' lives.'

'How many people were hurt?'

'Amazingly not many. Jon was one of them, and the coach driver of course.'

'And the driver of the car?'

'He was killed. So no one knows what was in his mind, whether he had a stroke, or a heart attack, or something. Jon was sitting right near the front,' she gulped.

'Oh, poor Jon.'

'It was fortunate that the coach was travelling in the centre of Edinburgh at the time. If they had been on a faster road, I dread to think what could have happened.'

Marina was beginning to feel a little reassured. It was bad there had been a crash, but it could have been so much worse. She was puzzled, though, as to why Jon would want to see her.

'Will you come and see him?' Mrs Bentley was asking.

'I don't know if that's such a good idea. Jon and I aren't together any more, you know.'

'I don't think you understand. I probably haven't made myself clear. I'm in such a state, I don't know what I'm saying. Jon hit his head. He was unconscious for a couple of days, and since he's come round, he seems to have lost part of his memory. He has no recollection of the accident, or of going to Australia.'

'His memory will come back, won't it?' Marina asked.

'We hope so, but it may take a while. At the moment, he's confused. He recognises me and his father, but he keeps saying, 'Where's Marina? Why isn't she here?' And I don't know how to answer him.'

'Oh dear. I'm so sorry.'

'Will you come? Please Marina. It might help if he sees you.'

'But if he thinks we're still together, it won't help if I tell him we split up.'

'You don't have to tell him that at first.'

'I can't lie to him.'

'You don't have to lie. You just have to be careful what you say.'

'He doesn't remember going to Australia?'

'No.'

'Shouldn't you tell him?'

'I did. I just told him that he'd been working in Australia, and been on holiday in Scotland, but he didn't seem to take it in. The doctors have told us not to mention it again for a few days. They think he might suddenly start remembering things. That would be better for him than us going into great detail about what happened.'

'Does he understand why he is in hospital?'

'He knows he's been in an accident, but he's not questioning us about it. He just keeps asking for you. Please come, Marina.'

'Look, Mrs Bentley, this has all been a bit of a shock for me. Can I think about it and ring you back later, when I've decided what to do?'

'Okay. I realise you must be very upset. We are too, but my husband and I would be so grateful if you could come to Edinburgh. I'm sure it would make a difference to Jon.'

Marina promised to ring them back

the next day when she'd had time to think and make plans.

She spent the rest of the evening and most of the night pondering it. What should she do? She had no intention of getting involved with Jon again, especially now she'd met Roberto. But on the other hand, she couldn't just be callous and ignore his mother's pleas. She thought it would be difficult to get time off work right now, as they were so busy, but maybe she could fly there on Saturday morning, find somewhere to stay overnight and return home Sunday evening? That way, there'd be no need for her to take time off work.

Of course, she'd have to tell her father what she was doing, just in case there were any problems and she couldn't get back to work for Monday morning. Then there was Roberto. How would he react when she told him? She wouldn't be able to see him on Saturday, as they'd arranged. She guessed that wouldn't go down too well. He'd want to know why she was suddenly flying off to Scotland. What should she say? If she told Roberto about Jon, he'd think she was standing him up to visit an ex-boyfriend. But Jon was a sick man. She couldn't just abandon him because she was going out with someone new. Marina hoped Roberto would be understanding, but in reality, she had no idea how he would take the news.

Early the next morning, before she set off for work, Marina rang Jon's parents.

Mrs Bentley answered the phone. 'I'm so glad you've rung. What's your decision?'

'I'll come to see Jon on Saturday and return home on Sunday.'

'Such a brief visit?'

'I can't do more than that. We're very busy at work. I'm not able to have time off at the moment.'

'What about compassionate leave? Couldn't you have that?'

'No.'

'But Jon was your boyfriend,' Mrs

Bentley persisted.

'He was, but he isn't now.'

'When you see him, you might decide to get back together. This accident could bring you closer. My husband and I always thought you two were well suited. We were very upset when you split up. Besides, Jon thinks you are his girlfriend.'

'Mrs Bentley, that's all in the past. I have no intention of getting back with Jon, and I'm sure that when he recovers, he will feel the same way.'

'You sound very definite about that.'

'I am.'

'Does that mean you've met someone else?'

Marina ignored Mrs Bentley's question, instead saying, 'When Jon went to Australia, we decided to go our separate ways. Now, Mrs Bentley, I can't talk any longer. I'll be late for work. I'll go to Edinburgh on Saturday and return home on Sunday. That's all I can do.'

'Okay, thank you. I'll meet you at the airport if you let me know what flight you're on. You will be flying, I take it?'

'Yes. If you let me know your mobile number, I'll text you when I've booked the flights.'

'Have you got anywhere to stay, Marina?'

'No. I'll look for somewhere later.'

'I'll get a room for you in my hotel. They're not full up. I'll pay, as it's my idea you come out to see Jon.'

'That's very kind, but I can't impose on you like that.'

'You're not imposing. I want to pay.'

'We'll see. It's just for Saturday night, though,' Marina reminded Mrs Bentley.

They exchanged mobile numbers and Marina hung up, wondering if she had done the right thing. Should she be going to Scotland? If Jon was still suffering from memory loss and had forgotten what had happened in the past, would it make things more confusing for him in the long run?

Mrs Bentley seemed quite certain that she should see him — but that was probably more to do with the fact that she was hoping they would get back together, Marina mused. Not that that would ever happen.

It had become clear to Marina, since meeting Roberto, that what she had felt for Jon was more akin to friendship. This made her pause. Did that mean she had fallen in love with Roberto? She'd known him such a short time, but he was constantly in her thoughts. She'd never felt that way about Jon. She'd enjoyed his company and liked going out with him, but that was all. And when the time came for him to leave, she'd been upset, but not heartbroken. By comparison, the thought of Roberto finishing with her was something she didn't even want to contemplate.

As soon as Marina arrived at the office, before starting on her work, she booked a flight out to Edinburgh for Saturday morning, and a return one for Sunday evening. She was not looking forward to it, and was dreading telling Roberto that she wouldn't be able to see him on Saturday.

During the morning, she received a brief text message from him.

Looking forward to seeing you on Saturday. Hope you are well. Have done lots of painting. Roberto.

Now Marina was in a quandary. She was pleased he had contacted her, and wanted to reply to his text, but what could she say? How could she explain everything in a text? It couldn't be done. She'd have to ring Roberto that evening. It was not going to be easy. Would he be understanding?

Marina was very busy again that day, and was late leaving the office. As soon as she arrived home, she quickly prepared a salad for herself and then telephoned her father.

'It's lovely to hear from you Marina,' he exclaimed. 'How are you?'

'I'm fine, Dad, but I thought I should let you know that I'm going away on Saturday. I hope to be back late on Sunday night, but I wanted to mention it, just in case.'

'Oh,' he paused. 'Is it a weekend away with Roberto? Bit soon, isn't it? After all, you haven't known him very long.'

'No, Dad. I am not going away with Roberto.'

'Where are you going then? It's not a secret, is it?'

'It's not a secret. I'm going to Edinburgh.'

'Sightseeing with a friend?'

'I'm visiting someone in hospital.'

'Oh dear. Someone I know? One of your girlfriends? I didn't know you knew anyone in Scotland.'

Her dad was in full Spanish Inquisition mode again, she thought. It would be even worse when she had to tell Roberto.

'You don't know all my friends,' she snapped.

'Sorry. I shouldn't be so nosey. It's none of my business. So, I guess you're letting me know in case there's any problem and you can't get back in time for work on Monday? Is that it?'

'Yes, that's right. I'm sorry, Dad, I shouldn't have snapped at you.' She sighed. 'I'm going to see Jon.'

'Jon? I thought you and he split up when he went to Australia?'

'We did.'

'So why are you going to see him, and what's he doing in Edinburgh?'

'It's a long story,' Marina sighed again. 'He's been in an accident and lost his memory. His mother called and begged me to go and see him. He keeps asking for me.'

'Tricky. Does he still think you're his girlfriend?'

'Apparently so.'

'How badly hurt is he?'

'Quite badly, I think. I'll find out when I get there.'

'I hope the poor chap recovers.'

'So do I.'

'It's going to be difficult for you if he thinks you're still his girlfriend.'

'Exactly.'

'Are you sure you should be going?'

'I'm not sure at all, but Mrs Bentley

kept pleading with me, and I didn't have the heart to refuse.'

'Does Roberto know you're going?'

'No, not yet.'

'Oh dear. I wonder what he'll say. He may not take kindly to your going off to see an ex-boyfriend.'

That was just what Marina had feared, but she hadn't expected her father to think the same way. Out loud, though, she said, 'I don't have to ask Roberto's permission to do anything.'

'No, of course you don't. If you're going Saturday morning and returning Sunday evening, will that be long enough? It's a long way to go for such a short while. I could try to sort out some cover at work so you could stay a bit longer, if you like?'

'I don't want to stay longer. I don't actually want to go at all. I'm only doing it to satisfy Mrs Bentley.'

'Okay. I really think you should tell Roberto as soon as possible, though.'

'I intend to, as soon as I've finished talking to you. I wanted to put you in the picture first.'

'Thank you. Well, good luck with the phone call. Let me know what Roberto has to say about it.'

'We've only just started going out together, so he probably won't say much at all.' Marina crossed her fingers. 'I'll be in touch when I get back from Edinburgh. Bye, Dad.'

She made herself a mug of coffee, took a few sips, plucked up courage and rang Roberto's mobile. There was no reply and it went to voicemail, asking her to leave a message. She hadn't expected this and didn't know what to say. Maybe he was working late and couldn't answer.

'Oh . . . er . . . Roberto? It's Marina. I need to talk to you. Can you ring me back, as soon as possible please?'

She hung up, wondering whether he would get her message. What if he didn't ring back? She couldn't just go away without telling him.

She switched on the television and tried to get interested in a film, but her mind kept wandering and she was unable to follow the plot. How would Roberto react? What would he say? Just when everything had been going so well! That seemed to be the story of her life. A series of traumatic events. Her mother becoming ill, and dying when Marina had barely become an adult; Jon going to Australia; the shock of her father's sudden marriage; and now Jon's accident.

After meeting Roberto, Marina had hoped life would get better. But now, she was fearful about what he would think when he heard she was visiting Jon. Did she have to say who she was visiting? Could she just say it was a friend? No. He would want to know which friend.

Marina was about to get ready for bed when her mobile sounded. She picked it up nervously.

'Hello, Marina. Sorry I missed your call. Had to work an extra shift today. Hope I'm not ringing too late, but you said you needed to talk to me?'

'That's right, I'm very sorry, but I can't go out with you on Saturday after all.'

'What a shame. How come?'

Marina gulped. 'I . . . I have to visit a friend. In Edinburgh. I've got to go on Saturday morning and come back Sunday evening.'

'Does it have to be this weekend?'

'My friend's had a serious accident.'

'I'm so sorry. What sort of accident?'

'A coach crash.'

'That's bad. Couldn't you get a couple of days off work to see her?'

'No, we're too busy.'

Roberto was not making it easy for her. She'd been afraid this would happen. Although, to be fair, she was doling out information as though it were hen's teeth, so he was bound to keep asking questions. Why hadn't she just explained properly, right from the start?

'Edinburgh's a long way,' he said.

'I know. I'm sorry if I've spoilt your plans.'

'It's not that. I'm thinking of you, having to make that journey on your own.'

'I'll be all right.'

'I've had an idea. Do you want some company? I'm free all this weekend. I could come with you.'

Marina gulped. 'That's very kind, but you don't need to do that.'

'I don't mind. I could do with a mini break.'

'No. I don't think that's a good idea.'

'You don't want me to come?' Roberto asked.

'It's not that, but I'll be busy. With my friend.'

'I just thought you might have liked someone to talk to on the journey, and to accompany you to the hospital.'

'It's very kind of you Roberto, but I'm meeting my friend's parents when I get there, and staying at their hotel. They persuaded me to go.'

'Okay, I know when I'm not wanted.'

'I don't want to upset you, but it really is better if I go on my own.'

'You win. By the way, does your friend have a name?'

'It . . . It's Jon.'

'Jon? A friend? Or your boyfriend?' he guessed, his voice cold.

'No. I mean, he was my boyfriend, but we split up some time ago. His mother pleaded with me to go so much that I couldn't refuse. He keeps asking to see me.'

Marina was trying to stop the tears which were threatening to flow.

'If you've split up, why would he want to see you? That doesn't make sense.'

'But . . . he's . . . '

'The truth is,' Roberto interrupted, 'you've chosen him instead of me.'

'It's not like that.'

'Isn't it? That's the way I see it. You've been letting me think that you were interested in me, when all the time you were hankering after your ex.' His voice rose to a crescendo.

'No . . . '

'I suppose you thought going out

with me was better than being on your own, but as soon as your ex clicked his fingers, you decided to go running back to him.'

'That's not true. Please, listen to me, Roberto.'

'I've heard enough. I'm glad I found out about you before we got too involved. Goodbye, Marina.'

7

'Listen, Roberto,' Marina pleaded. 'You've got to listen to me.'

But it was too late; he'd hung up.

She burst into tears of frustration, tinged with anger and anguish. Why hadn't Roberto listened? He'd passed judgement and given her no chance to explain. She'd feared this would happen, but had hoped she was wrong. Perhaps she should have told him about the telephone call she'd received from Jon's mother, and discussed it with him, before going ahead and booking the flight to Edinburgh? Or just told him the whole story, right from the start. It was too late, now, though, to speculate on what she should or should not have done. She had to live with the consequences of her actions.

Roberto had sounded so angry. It felt unjust. She'd been trying to do her best for everyone: helping Jon, pleasing his parents, not inconveniencing her work colleagues, and being fair to Roberto — but he didn't believe her.

So, that's the end of another brief romance, she told herself, when finally her tears had ceased. They'd hardly got started, and now it was all over. Maybe it was for the best. If he had such a low opinion of her, and was ready to think the worst, then she was better off without him. After all, she'd only known him a short time. She'd have to get on with her life and forget about Roberto. But that was not going to be easy.

* * *

On Saturday morning, she set off early for her trip to Scotland. She had a good flight, and Mr and Mrs Bentley were there at the airport to meet her. They both looked older than she remembered, and rather haggard, but that was to be expected, with all the worry they'd had.

'I'm so glad to see you,' Jon's mother said, as she gave Marina a kiss on the cheek. 'We've hired a car for the next few days. It makes life easier. We'll take you to the hotel to freshen up, and then later on we'll drive you to the hospital.'

'Yes, it's good of you to come,' Mr Bentley added, picking up Marina's travel bag.

She followed them out of the airport and into the car park. Soon they were on their way to the hotel.

'How is Jon?' Marina enquired.

'The doctors say he's doing well, but it doesn't seem that way to me,' said his mother.

'What do you mean?'

'Well, it's his memory. He still can't remember anything about the accident.'

'But the doctors say he will in time. We just have to be patient,' Mr Bentley replied.

'He seems to be living in the past,' Mrs Bentley went on. 'He knows nothing about his time in Australia and still thinks . . . '

'That I'm his girlfriend,' Marina interrupted.

'I'm afraid so.'

'We can't let him believe that,' Marina insisted. 'It's not true.'

'The doctors have said we shouldn't upset him. Please be careful what you say to him, Marina.'

'I will try, but I can't tell lies.'

'No, but you can be . . . er . . . economical with the truth,' Mr Bentley joined in. 'Don't tell him you split up. Don't mention Australia. Just talk about your job and how busy you are, and ask him about the hospital and what the nurses are like. You know, just general things. Be as cheerful as you can. But I'd better warn you, he doesn't look too good. Has quite a lot of cuts and bruises. Don't show him you're upset.'

'I will try to be tactful,' Marina promised. This was going to be really hard. She wasn't the world's best actress.

'I expect you could do with something to eat. I'm starving,' Mrs Bentley remarked, after Marina had checked in at the hotel. 'We missed our breakfast this morning, coming to the airport.'

'Oh, I'm sorry. You should have let me get a taxi to the hotel.'

'No, of course not. You're our guest. We asked you to come here. It's the least we can do, picking you up and sorting out a meal.'

'You are very kind,' Marina murmured.

'Now, why don't you go to your room and freshen up while we see what's available?'

'I'm not really hungry.'

'I'll see if they can do some bacon sandwiches. You must eat something. We'll wait here for you.'

'That'll be fine. One sandwich will be plenty for me, thank you.'

The hotel porter carried Marina's bag to the lift and escorted her to a room on the sixth floor.

She quickly refreshed herself, sent a

brief text message to her father telling him she had arrived safely, and then went down to Reception.

'We'll go into the bar,' Mr Bentley told her. 'They'll serve us in there. By the way, you don't have to be formal with us. I'm Cecil, and my wife is Barbara.'

One hour later, they were back in the car on their way to the hospital. Marina was feeling not only extremely nervous, but also quite queasy. She regretted finishing the sandwiches which Jon's parents had ordered for her. They had eaten frugally but insisted that she tuck in.

'Eat up,' Barbara had said. 'You look as if you need building up.'

That was the last thing she needed, Marina thought, but she had been too polite to refuse and had eaten the sandwiches valiantly.

'You can visit any time between ten in the morning and eight o'clock in the evening,' Cecil informed Marina as they were driving along. 'We usually stay most of the day, just popping out for some refreshments.'

'That's nice for Jon. He must be so glad to see you.'

'Yes, but it's you he wants to see. He keeps asking for you. He can't understand why you haven't come before.'

'What have you said about me?'

'I reminded him that you're working all the week, and that Scotland is a long way from home, but you would come when you could.'

'Thanks. But sooner or later he will have to be told. About us, I mean,' Marina insisted.

'Not yet. It's too soon. There's plenty of time.'

'We don't know when his memory will come back. We can't deceive Jon. It's not fair on him,' Marina answered. 'I think we should have another word with the doctor and explain the situation.'

'Marina's got a point,' Cecil put in. 'Let's try to speak to a doctor today.'

'You'll be lucky to see one at the

weekend,' Barbara replied. 'Besides, they won't be able to tell us any more than they did before.'

It was almost as if Barbara didn't want Jon to get his memory back. Suddenly, it became clear to her: Barbara didn't want Jon to go back to Australia! She was pleased to have him back in the country, and was probably hoping that if his memory was slow in returning, he would decide to stay in England.

Cecil parked his car, and Marina followed Jon's parents through double glass doors into the main hospital building, where scores of people were milling around. They took the lift, walked along a vast corridor, and arrived outside the ward. Barbara pressed a buzzer and the door opened. They passed the nurses' station, where several members of staff were sitting staring at computers. They entered a small side room, where four patients were sitting propped up in bed, all with bandages or plasters on their heads.

Marina stifled a cry of shock as she realised that the occupant of the bed nearest the door was Jon. Cecil had warned her that he looked different, but she wasn't prepared for what she saw. The top of Jon's head was wrapped in a bandage, and his face was badly swollen and bruised. His eyes were dull and he was staring straight ahead, seemingly unaware of his surroundings.

'Jon,' she murmured.

There was no response.

'He's getting depressed,' Barbara whispered to Marina. 'He can't understand what's happening to him.'

Barbara and Cecil walked over to him, and Cecil patted Jon's arm.

'Hello, Son,' Cecil said.

Barbara bent down and put her face close to his. 'Look who's come to see you.'

She pointed to Marina.

He moved his head lethargically, faced her, and then gasped as if he had suddenly come back to life. 'Marina!'

'Thank God,' Barbara murmured.

'You recognise her.'

'You've come at last. Where have you been?' His voice was low and husky.

'Cecil, let's go and get ourselves a drink.' Barbara grabbed hold of his arm. 'You two have a chat. We'll be back soon.'

'That's a good idea.' Cecil followed his wife out of the ward.

Marina's heart sank. She didn't want to be left on her own with Jon. What could she say? She was horrified by his appearance, and felt deeply sorry for him. She didn't want to upset him more. She would have to be diplomatic and try to steer the conversation away from discussions about their relationship, but she knew that diplomacy was not her strong point. Maybe she should explain the situation to his doctor and ask for some advice. She didn't want to do or say anything that would impede his progress. Jon's parents had said they would try to speak to a doctor. All this flashed through Marina's mind as Jon reached out his hand towards her.

'Come closer. Let me look at you,' he murmured.

She leaned over the bed and gently took his hand. 'I'm so sorry about the accident,' she whispered.

'You look even more beautiful than I remembered.'

Marina blushed.

'I hope you aren't too shocked by my appearance. I know I'm a sight,' Jon continued.

'No, you're not. When your cuts and bruises heal, you'll be back to your old self.' That might not be true, but what else could she say?

'Oh, I'm so glad you've come. I was beginning to think you didn't want to see me anymore.'

'What do you remember about the accident?' Marina asked, trying to change the conversation.

'Nothing much. Apparently I was on a coach, sitting near the front when it happened, but I don't know why I was on it.'

'You were having a holiday.'

'So my Mum says. Don't let's talk about that. There are more important things to discuss now you're here.'

'We should talk about it,' Marina insisted. 'It's important you try to remember things. It must be terrible, forgetting so much.'

'What do you think I've been doing for the past few days since the accident?' Jon snapped. 'I've been trying to remember, but it's impossible.'

'I'm sorry. I didn't mean to upset you.'

'I'm not.' He squeezed her hand. 'Marina . . . could you bear to kiss my ugly face?'

She bent down, let go of his hand and gently kissed his cheek, avoiding his cut and swollen lips.

'Thank you. I think everything will be all right now you're here. How long can you stay? I guess you've had to take time off work?'

'I'm afraid I have to go back home tomorrow evening, but I'll come again to see you before I leave.'

'So soon?'

'I can't take time off work at the moment.'

'Not even if you explain that your boyfriend's had an accident and is in hospital?'

'No. What's the last thing you remember?' Marina tried one more time to change the subject.

'I'm not sure. I do remember sitting in a . . . I suppose it was a concert hall — I think I was with you — and hearing all this loud music. It sounded like guns firing.'

'Oh Jon, that's brilliant. We were at a concert. They were playing Tchaikovsky's Eighteen Twelve Overture.'

'You remember it too?'

'Yes. You were with me.'

'When was it?'

'Quite a while ago. Maybe nine months, or even longer.' Before Jon had decided to go to Australia, Marina thought. 'You see your memory is coming back.'

'I suppose so.' Jon sounded doubtful.

'Someone said I was working in Australia, but I can't believe that. Why would I have left you and gone there? Anyway, I don't want to talk about that. While I have been lying here in bed I've had time to think about . . . '

'But you should talk about it,' Marina interrupted. 'You need to start remembering things.'

Before he could say any more, his parents returned.

'Everything okay?' Barbara asked.

'Yes, fine. It's so good to see Marina again, but she tells me she has to go back home tomorrow evening.'

'That's right, Son.'

'You'll come again though?'

She was spared from answering by Barbara, who replied, 'Jon, it costs a fortune to keep flying here. We'll have to see what can be arranged when you come out of hospital. You'll probably need a few weeks' rest and recuperation before . . . before you think about returning to work. You can stay with us.'

Marina smiled gratefully at Barbara,

but she wondered if Jon would be able to return to work. If his memory didn't improve, he certainly wouldn't be able to go back to Australia. Then she chided herself; she was being too pessimistic. Of course he would get better and work again, even if it was only back in England.

'I hadn't thought of that. I keep forgetting I'm in Scotland. If only I could remember more.' Jon touched his bandaged head.

'You will in time, Son.'

They spent the rest of the day together at the hospital, but as Barbara had predicted, they were not able to see a doctor. They did manage to make an appointment for Jon's parents to see one on Monday, though.

'We'll let you know what the doctor says,' Barbara promised Marina.

After leaving the hospital, Jon's parents took Marina into the hotel restaurant for dinner and insisted on paying for everything, including the accommodation bill.

'It really was good of you to come,' Cecil remarked. 'You didn't have to, as you and Jon are no longer together, but I think it has helped him already, seeing you. He really perked up this afternoon. He's been so down the past few days. I was getting worried that he'd lost the will to get better.'

'Oh, surely not.' Marina couldn't believe that.

'I thought the same thing,' Barbara agreed. 'That was why I telephoned. If anyone can help Jon, it's you.'

Marina was in a difficult position. She didn't want to give him or his parents false hope.

'Look, Barbara — I can't pretend to be his girlfriend. That wouldn't be right.'

'Not even if it helped Jon recover?'

'He would have to find out some time. It might make matters worse.'

'It couldn't be much worse,' Barbara said bitterly.

'It could, Dear,' Cecil replied, taking hold of her hand across the table.

'Yes, I suppose it could.' She gripped his fingers.

'We've got to be positive.'

'You're right, Cecil.' Barbara turned to Marina. 'Will you promise me something?'

'What's that?'

'When you see Jon tomorrow, please don't mention it. He looked so much better this afternoon, we don't want him to have a relapse.'

'Okay. I'll try not to say anything.'

'Thanks Marina. We will be seeing the doctor on Monday,' Cecil joined in. 'We'll ask him if he thinks Jon should be told yet.'

★ ★ ★

That night, as Marina lay in her hotel bed, she found it hard to relax. Sleep wouldn't come. She was reliving the events of the past few days. She felt she had done the right thing for Jon in coming to see him. She'd seen for herself how he had livened up after her arrival. By the time she left, he was quite chirpy. She hoped that her visit the next day would go equally well, and she wouldn't be forced to tell lies.

At the back of her mind, though, was her last conversation with Roberto and how he had judged her so harshly. That hurt. Could she forgive him for that? Would she ever get the chance to forgive him? And more importantly, did she want to?

8

The next morning after breakfast, Marina telephoned her father.

'How was Jon?' Lionel enquired.

'I think he looks awful. He's covered in cuts and bruises. His head's bandaged up, but according to his parents, he's much better. They feared he was losing hope, but he seemed to cheer up during the day.'

'That was probably because you were there.'

'I know. He still thinks we're together. Jon's mother made me promise not to say anything until after they had spoken to the doctor, but that's not until Monday, after I've gone home.'

'It must be very difficult for you.'

'It is. Extremely. I'm scared I'll say something I shouldn't.'

'You'll be okay. You can be very tactful with some of our awkward clients.'

'But this is different. I really don't want to do anything which will hinder Jon's progress. It's hard seeing him in so much distress. I can't upset him.'

'I'm sure you won't do that.'

'I'll try not to.'

'How did Roberto take it, when you told him you were going to Scotland?'

'Badly, I'm afraid. He . . . he finished with me.'

'Oh no! That's terrible. What's the matter with the man? I don't know him very well, but I thought better of him than that. I guessed he wouldn't be happy, but I never imagined he would do that.'

'He didn't give me a chance to explain.'

'Maybe when he thinks about it, he will calm down and get in touch to apologise.'

'I'm not sure about that. Even if he does, do I want to get involved with someone who is likely to over-react to every little thing?'

'I can't answer that, Marina. It

depends on how much you like him.'

Too much, Marina thought, but she replied, 'I can't worry about that now. I've got to cope with seeing Jon today, and that's not going to be easy.'

'I'll have a word with Amelia. See what she thinks about Roberto. She's known him since they were children. She might be able to put in a good word for you.'

'No, don't do that,' Marina said quickly. That was the last thing she wanted, her father involving Amelia, especially if her suspicions about the past involvement were correct. 'Please don't discuss what I have told you with anyone,' she begged. 'I can sort out my own affairs thank you.'

'Okay, if that's what you want.'

'It is. I'll let you know when I get back,' Marina promised.

'I hope seeing Jon today goes well.'

'So do I.'

⋆ ⋆ ⋆

An hour later, Jon's parents escorted Marina to the hospital. Cecil led the way into the ward, followed by Barbara, with Marina lagging behind. She was dreading it. What were they going to talk about all day?

Cecil and Barbara planned to have lunch together. 'We'll leave the young people on their own. They won't want us tagging along the whole time,' Barbara had said. 'We don't often have Sunday lunch out. It'll be good for us.'

Not so good for me, Marina was thinking. She'd been thrown in at the deep end. At least yesterday, she had only been left with Jon for a short while.

They found Jon sitting in an armchair beside his bed, looking much more alert.

'You look better, Son,' Cecil remarked. 'It's nice to see you out of bed. How are you feeling?'

'Hello, Dad. I don't feel too bad today. My head's not quite so painful, and my legs are getting stronger. I walked all around the ward this morning without any help. The nurse said I'm doing really well.'

'That's wonderful.' Barbara kissed her son and perched on the end of his bed. 'Cecil, get a chair for Marina.'

'Yes, of course.'

'Marina, so glad you're here,' Jon exclaimed, leaning forward, stretching out his arms to hug her as she stood stiffly in front of him. 'Aren't you going to kiss me?'

'It's nice to see you too,' she murmured, trying to sound as if she meant it, as she gave him a peck on the cheek. Her mind was in a turmoil. She found this situation embarrassing. Jon was gazing at her in a way that she found disturbing. She was itching to tell him that she was no longer his girlfriend, but didn't want to break her promise to Barbara. If only they could see a doctor today so that the matter could be clarified. Was it better for Jon himself to try to remember the past? Or should they explain things to him?

Although Marina was pleased to see that Jon was improving, she was not looking forward to the next few hours.

For a while, they all chatted about the hospital, the staff and Jon's treatment. Marina sat quietly, listening, and trying to avoid eye contact with him.

Then Cecil said, 'Come along, Barbara, I think it's time we had our lunch. I've booked a table for us.'

'Lovely.' She kissed Jon. 'I hope you two have a good afternoon.' She turned to Marina. 'We'll be back in time to take you to the hotel to collect your things before your flight.'

'Thank you.'

'If you get hungry, Marina, the café downstairs is quite good. We often go there while Jon has a little nap.'

'I won't want to nap today,' he replied, before she could say anything. 'I want to make the most of my time with Marina.'

'You've got to let the poor girl get

something to eat,' Cecil answered.

'Of course, but she can bring it up here.'

Jon watched as his parents walked out of the ward.

'At last, I've got you to myself,' he murmured. 'I thought they were never going to leave. You look lovely today, Marina, even more gorgeous than yesterday. That's one thing I haven't forgotten — your beautiful, long, blonde hair. It's always just perfect.'

'I'm not so sure about that,' she replied blushing. He hadn't spoken to her like this when they'd been together! The blow to his head must have changed him. He was much more down to earth previously. He wouldn't have said romantic things like that.

'You're seeing me through rose-coloured spectacles,' she told him.

'No. You are the most attractive girl I've ever known. Don't sit so far away. Come closer Marina.'

Reluctantly, she pushed her chair nearer to the bed. It was all getting too personal. She didn't know how to handle it.

'What are the nurses like?' she asked, trying to change the subject. 'Are they kind?'

'Very nice. I told you that.'

'So you did. Sorry.' Marina rummaged in her bag and pulled out a couple of paper bags. She put them on the bed in front of Jon. 'I've brought you fruit and a packet of chocolate biscuits.'

'Thank you. That's very kind. I'll eat some tonight after you've left. I wish you didn't have to go. Couldn't you ring up your office and say you've been delayed?'

'No Jon. I've told you. I can't do that. It would be letting too many people down.' That was true, but not the real reason she wasn't staying.

'You're too conscientious.'

'Not really. I just know how it puts everyone out if someone stays away from the office unexpectedly.'

'What happens if you're ill?'

'That's a different matter. Nothing can be done about that.'

'Okay. Just promise me you'll come and see me again soon.'

Marina couldn't do that, so didn't know how to answer. 'We'll see,' she murmured. 'Now, tell me what treatment you're having.'

For the next two hours Marina managed to keep Jon talking about the hospital and the care he was receiving. Every time he tried to steer the conversation away to more personal matters, she managed to avoid a difficult situation, either by getting him to talk about some other aspect of hospital life, or by reminding him of things they had done together when they had first met. Most of these he remembered, but he had no recollection of the events leading up to him going to Australia.

'I think it's time you got yourself something to eat and drink,' Jon said when his afternoon tea came round. 'I'm sorry I've kept you talking so long, but it's lovely to have you here. I've missed you so much Marina.'

'I'll go and get a snack,' she replied, feeling relieved that at last she could have a break. She had found it hard to be with him so long and pretend that they were still together. She was definitely not cut out to be an actress! 'You can have a little rest. I've probably worn you out with all my chatter.'

'No. I feel so much better for seeing you.' He reached out his hands towards her. 'Can you give me a kiss before you go, while we are on our own? My parents will probably be back soon.'

Marina didn't want to upset him so she bent down and briefly kissed his cheek, but Jon pulled her closer. 'I know I don't look very good, and you were horrified when you saw me, but I'm still the same inside. I won't always look this bad, I hope. Could you bear to give me a proper kiss. You are my girlfriend, after all Marina.'

Now what could she do? She didn't

want to kiss him, but neither did she want to do anything that might hinder his recovery.

As his arms went around her they were startled by a deep voice saying, 'Sorry to disturb you two. It's time to take your blood pressure, Mr Bentley.'

She pulled away quickly feeling so relieved. She'd been saved by the nurse, who was standing, grinning, at the end of the bed.

'I'll go and get something to eat,' she muttered, feeling hot and embarrassed.

'Don't be too long,' Jon called.

Marina followed the signs to the hospital café, purchased a coffee and a dish of pasta and found a table by herself. She wasn't all that hungry, but felt she should eat something. She was tired and stressed from the ordeal of the past few days. She briefly wondered what Roberto was doing, but quickly dismissed the thought from her mind. What he did now was no concern of hers. They were finished. He'd made that clear.

She was just drinking her coffee when she heard her mobile phone bleeping. Assuming it was a text from her dad, wanting to know how she was getting on, she decided to look at it later. Briefly, she hoped once more that he hadn't told Amelia anything. She glanced at her watch. Not too long now before her flight home. She supposed she'd better get back to Jon.

When she returned to the ward, she was relieved to see that Jon's parents had come back.

'Hello, Marina,' said Cecil. 'Jon's been getting impatient for you.'

'Sorry. I had to queue up quite a while.' That was not completely true. There had been a queue, but she hadn't waited that long. She was annoyed with herself. This whole business was making her tell lies, something she was not in the habit of doing.

'You seemed to be gone ages,' Jon moaned.

'I'm sorry. Good for you to have had a rest, though.'

'I'm not tired. Anyway come and sit down.'

'Did you have a nice lunch?' Marina asked Jon's parents.

'Lovely, thanks,' Barbara replied.

'How was your blood pressure?' Marina enquired of Jon.

'The nurse said it had gone up a bit, so I told him that was because my gorgeous girlfriend had come to see me, and he said, 'Yes you've picked a good one there'.'

Cecil and Barbara laughed, but Marina cringed with embarrassment. They knew the situation, she fumed, yet they seemed to be encouraging Jon to believe something false. She supposed they would like it to be true. It would make life easier for all of them.

Marina's phone bleeped again.

'Was that your mobile?' Jon asked.

'Yes. It's probably just Dad.'

'Shouldn't you look at it?'

Maybe she should — her dad was

being very insistent. She hoped it was nothing urgent.

'You go ahead, see what he wants. I don't mind,' Jon assured her.

'Okay.'

Barbara pulled a newspaper from her bag and passed it to her son as Marina looked at her phone. There were two messages, but they were not from her father. They were from Roberto.

'Is everything all right?' Jon asked, staring at Marina, who suddenly found she was shaking. She hadn't expected this. She'd wanted to hear from Roberto, of course, but had believed him when he said it was all over.

I'm very sorry for the terrible things I said. I hope you can forgive me. Please ring me when you get back. Roberto

Marina didn't look at the second text. She'd save that for later.

'Er . . . yes, thanks.' She tried hard to pull herself together.

'Was it your Dad?'

'No, just a friend. I'll send a reply later.' She forced a smile.

'I don't seem to have your mobile number,' Jon told her. 'My phone was wrecked in the coach crash, so they tell me. Can you let me have it? Then I can text you when you're back home.'

She tore a page from her notebook and wrote it down. It couldn't do any harm — he wouldn't want to contact her when he found out the truth.

'We haven't got too much longer,' Barbara said to Marina. 'Come on Cecil. Let's get ourselves a cup of tea. Leave them alone for a few minutes.'

'A good idea. We'll be back in the morning, Jon. Got to see what the doctor has to say.'

'Okay. See you then.'

Barbara turned to Marina. 'We'll meet you downstairs by the main entrance in twenty minutes.'

They waved to their son as they walked away.

Jon watched until they were out of sight. Then he held out his arms towards Marina. 'Come here. I want to talk to you.'

She did as he asked, wondering what he had to say. Was it about their past? Maybe he was going to try to persuade her to visit him again.

'What is it Jon?'

He took hold of her hands. 'I've had a lot of time to think since I've been in hospital. I know my memory is very bad, but the doctors think it will get a lot better in time, and my head and other injuries will heal, so I won't look quite so bad.'

'That's good, Jon.'

'Yes, but what I'm trying to say is this — I may not know what I was doing in Australia, or why I had come to Edinburgh for a holiday, but there's one thing I do know.'

'What's that?'

'I've missed you so much. I've no idea why I left you behind.'

'Don't worry about it, Jon.' This was getting too personal again.

'Let me finish, please, Marina. I don't want to waste any more time. I want us to be together, and I hope you do, too. So, I know this is not very romantic, but what I'm trying to say is — Marina, when I'm better . . . will you marry me?'

9

Marina threw her bag onto the floor and sank down into the window seat. She glanced along the aisle to see if anyone was heading for her row. Thankfully, it seemed no one was. She'd arrived just in time for the flight.

After the shock of her final few minutes with Jon, and her subsequent ordeal with his parents, she wanted to be on her own. She couldn't face having to make polite conversation with anyone. She closed her eyes, hoping that she wouldn't be disturbed. Her head was aching and buzzing with memories of the past few hours. She'd been taken completely unawares by Jon's proposal, and hadn't known how to respond. She'd probably said all the wrong things, given him hope when there was none, but her main aim was not to upset him. She'd seen how much better he looked since her arrival, and she didn't want to do or say anything that would impede his progress.

'Oh, Jon,' she'd replied. 'I . . . I never expected this. I don't know what to say.'

'Just say yes.'

'But we haven't seen each other for such a long while. You might change your mind when you feel better.'

'Why do you say that?'

'Because a lot has happened since . . . '

'Since I went to Australia. Is that what you're saying?'

'Yes.'

'I don't remember going. I've no idea why I was there, and I certainly don't want to go back. My life is here with you.'

'No, Jon, it isn't. You were happy in Australia.' Should she have said that? 'You will realise that soon, when your memory returns.'

'What if it never returns?'

'Don't say that.'

'I'm just being realistic.'

154

'You've got to be positive.'

'Now I've seen you again, I really don't care about my previous life. What's important is how we feel about each other, and the future. So, Marina, what's your answer? Will you marry me?'

'Jon, we can't decide anything now. It's all too soon. You must get better first.'

What else could she say? If she said no, it might cause him to have a relapse. She had to stall.

'So, you're turning me down?' He spoke slowly and quietly. All his animation had evaporated. His face suddenly looked haggard and grey. 'You're embarrassed by my appearance. That's what it is. I won't always look this bad, Marina. The doctors say I will hardly have any scars when my wounds have healed.'

'No, Jon. Of course I'm not embarrassed.'

'Then what is it? Why won't you accept my proposal?'

Marina felt she couldn't refuse him outright. She didn't know what harm that might do. 'I'm just saying we must wait until you have recovered, because you might feel differently then.'

'Okay, if that's what you want, Marina. We will wait a while. But I'm quite sure I won't change my mind.'

She was a cowardly hypocrite! She'd led him on. Given him false hope. She shouldn't have done that. How was she going to extricate herself from this dilemma? It was all Barbara's fault. She should never have made that promise to her. Deep down though, Marina knew she was being unfair to Barbara. After all, she was only doing what any mother would do, trying to aid her son's recovery.

Marina was brought out of her reverie by someone jostling her.

'So sorry, I've woken you up,' an elderly lady said, breathlessly, as she eased herself into the seat beside her. 'I can't do my belt up. My fingers are so bad. It's arthritis, you know.'

'Let me help you,' Marina replied. This was what she'd hoped to avoid, having to make polite conversation with a stranger, but she couldn't be rude and ignore the woman. 'I wasn't asleep. Just relaxing.' She leaned forward and did up the belt. 'There you are.'

'Thank you so much. It's very kind of you. I'm sorry to be a nuisance.'

'You're not.'

'Oh, we're taking off. I nearly missed this flight.'

'So did I,' Marina answered.

'My taxi didn't turn up,' the woman continued. 'Had to ring for another. Just made it in time. Heard the loudspeaker calling for all remaining passengers to board at once. I still haven't got my breath back.' She put her hand on her chest. 'My heart's pumping like mad.'

Marina looked at her, noting her florid face, which was getting paler.

'Do you want me to call the stewardess for you when the seatbelt signs go off?'

'No, I'll be all right in a minute.'

'If you're sure.'

'I shouldn't have hurried. The doctor told me to take it easy. My heart's not as good as it was.'

The plane lurched upwards. Marina was worried. The woman seemed to be gasping for breath. She could see her chest heaving up and down. All thoughts about Jon had gone from her mind. Now she had something more important to deal with. This woman was in trouble.

'Do you have any medication with you?'

'Yes . . . in . . . my bag.'

'Do you think you should take something?'

'Maybe. I don't feel good at all. Could you get it for me, dear?'

Marina rummaged in the pocket of the woman's bag, and found a bottle full of tiny tablets.

'Are these what you want?'

'Yes.'

Marina read the label and opened the

bottle. 'Here, put this under your tongue.'

'Thanks.'

She watched the elderly woman closely and was relieved to see the colour returning to her face.

'Is everything all right?' The stewardess was standing beside them. 'I could see something was wrong, but couldn't get out of my seat until the signs went off.'

'This lady is not feeling very well,' Marina told her.

'I'm better now, thanks to you.' She patted Marina's hand.

'Are you travelling together?'

'No, I'm on my own,' the elderly woman answered, 'but this young lady has very kindly taken care of me.'

'I haven't done much,' Marina protested.

'I suggest you shut your eyes and have a little nap,' the stewardess told the woman. 'It's not a long flight. You need to get your strength back for disembarking. Is anyone meeting you?'

'My son.'

'That's good.' She turned to Marina. 'Could you keep an eye on her for me, please?'

'Yes, of course.'

'If you get worried, don't hesitate to call me.'

'I won't.'

The woman lay back. Her breathing had eased, and her colour had returned.

Marina felt relieved, but couldn't settle down. She had to watch the woman in case she started feeling unwell again. Life was unpredictable, she mused. You never knew what was going to happen next. She'd intended sitting quietly on this flight, not communicating with anyone, but instead she'd ended up being a nursemaid to an elderly lady.

When Marina observed that the woman was sleeping peacefully, she relaxed a little and allowed her mind to wander back to the afternoon.

Jon's parents had returned soon after his proposal. She'd hoped he would say no more about it, but was horrified when he said, 'I've asked Marina to marry me.'

Cecil and Barbara stared from one to the other. 'You what?' Cecil spluttered.

'I've asked Marina . . . ' He stopped. 'Why are you staring at me like that?'

'Don't you think it's a bit soon?' his father asked.

'You should wait until your memory's come back,' Barbara added.

'That won't make any difference. I've told Marina that.'

'What did you answer?'

They all looked at Marina.

'I said we should wait.'

'Quite right,' Cecil replied. 'Jon, you've got to get yourself well again before you make any big decisions. You must be patient. Wait for your memory to come back.'

'And what if it doesn't? What if I stay like this?'

'That won't happen. You mustn't think that way.' Barbara wiped a tear from her eye.

'I do try to be positive, but it's not easy. I'm tired of being here in hospital, feeling so weak and helpless. I want things to be as before.'

'We want that too,' Barbara assured him. 'And they will be; but it will take time.'

Cecil looked at his watch. 'I'm sorry, Son. I don't want to rush away, but we've got to go. Me and your Mum will be back in the morning. Now, you remember what I've said. Take things easy. Don't expect too much, too soon. Come on, Marina, we don't want you to miss your flight.'

She bent down and kissed Jon's forehead.

'Come and visit me again soon,' he whispered. 'I love you. I'll text you later. Let me know when you get back home.'

'Bye, Jon. Get well soon. I'll keep in touch.' Now what had she let herself in for? Although, what else could she have done? She was in a very difficult position. Jon had said he loved her.

He'd never said that before. This blow to the head he'd suffered when the coach had crashed had done all sorts of things to his brain. He was a different person from the one she remembered. Would he ever go back to how he was previously? If he didn't, what would the future hold for him? And what did it hold for her? She knew hers didn't include Jon, but how was she going to make him realise that? And what was going to happen about Roberto? Life was so complicated!

On the way to the airport, Jon's parents had wanted to talk about his proposal.

'That must have come as a surprise,' Barbara remarked. 'You did the right thing, telling him to wait, though. I'm glad you didn't refuse him. After all, in a few weeks, you might feel differently about Jon. You may see things in a new light and want to get back with him.'

'It was hard for me. I didn't want to give him false hope, but I couldn't deliberately hurt him either. I won't change my mind, though, Barbara. I won't be marrying Jon.'

'You don't know how you'll feel when you've seen more of him. You two look so right together. He'll make a good husband. He's a very kind and thoughtful chap. When you think about it, I'm sure you'll see it my way.'

What was the use of arguing? Barbara wouldn't listen. She was so convinced that Marina should accept Jon's proposal. She was living in her own little dream world.

'Anyway, you will come and see him as often as you can, won't you? It will be easier for you once he comes out of hospital.'

'If I can.'

'Make sure you keep in touch.'

'I will, but that's all I can promise. I'm not going to discuss it any more, Barbara. Thank you for all your help. I'll ring you tomorrow evening to find out what the doctor said.'

'Okay.'

Cecil turned to his wife. 'Leave the

girl alone, Barbara. Stop browbeating her. Just be thankful she came to see Jon.'

When they arrived at the airport, it was time to check in, so Marina kissed them goodbye and headed for the desk. She breathed a sigh of relief as they waved and walked away. She had no time to read the messages from Roberto. They would have to wait until she got off the plane, she decided.

* * *

'Are we nearly there yet?' the elderly woman asked, bringing Marina back to the present.

'Won't be long. How are you feeling?'

'A lot better. That tablet worked a treat.'

'Good. If you like, I'll stay with you until we find your son. I don't need to rush. I'm not being met by anyone.'

'No boyfriend to meet you?'

'No.'

'I am surprised, a good-looking girl

like you. I'm sure it won't be long before you find someone.'

Marina smiled wryly, but said nothing. Someone did want her. Jon!

'That's very kind of you, anyway,' the woman said. 'My name is Emily, by the way.'

They sat chatting for the rest of the flight, and then Marina escorted Emily off the plane. They soon found her son. When they'd said their farewells, Marina sat down and picked up her phone to read Roberto's messages.

She re-read the first message.

I'm very sorry for the terrible things I said. I hope you can forgive me. Please ring me when you get back. Roberto

Then she scrolled through to the second one.

Please reply, Marina. I'm waiting to hear from you. Roberto.

Well, he'd have to continue to wait. She wasn't rushing to answer. She'd spent a miserable weekend, thinking that everything was over between them. Now he expected her to contact him immediately. She'd do it tomorrow, when she got home from work. She was too tired to have a long discussion tonight, and she was still in two minds about what she would say to him. She was glad he'd contacted her, of course, but she remained annoyed about the high-handed way he'd treated her.

10

When Marina arrived home, she quickly unpacked, had a snack and then telephoned her father.

'I'm back. How's everything with you?'

'We're okay, thanks. Been wondering how you've been getting on.'

'Well, I'm glad to be home. It's all been very stressful.'

'I'm sure it has. How's Jon?'

'He seemed a lot brighter on Sunday. I think he's making progress.' Marina didn't tell her father about Jon's proposal, although she would have loved to discuss it with someone. She knew, though, that he would tell his wife, and she didn't want Amelia getting involved. Marina still had a feeling that Amelia was not happy about her friendship with Roberto. She would probably be delighted if Marina got back together with Jon.

'Will you go and see him again?'

'I don't know. He asked me to, and his parents want me to, but visiting him might make matters worse. He still thinks we're together. He can remember nothing about his time in Australia, and has no idea why he was in Edinburgh.'

'That must be so difficult for you.'

'Precisely. You understand that, but his parents don't. Especially Barbara. She has visions of us getting back together, and living happily ever after. I tried telling her it wasn't going to happen, but she wouldn't listen.'

'Oh dear.'

'Dad, can I ask you to please not discuss this with Amelia.'

'Why not? She's my wife. I tell her everything.'

'Because it has nothing to do with her. It's a private matter, between me and Jon. You do see that?' she coaxed.

'Okay, Marina. To please you, I'll keep quiet. But I don't know why you're taking this attitude.'

'Thanks Dad. I just prefer it that way.'

'Did you hear from Roberto?'

'Yes, I had a couple of text messages. He's apologised.'

'That's good.'

'I suppose it is.'

'It's what you wanted.'

'Yes, but it's not going to be easy if he keeps flying off the handle over every little thing.'

'He was jealous, Marina.'

'There was nothing to be jealous of.'

'You knew that, but he didn't.'

'He should have trusted me. I haven't replied to his message yet. I'll ring him tomorrow. I need an early night, ready for work in the morning. I'm worn out with all the travelling, and the stress of seeing Jon so helpless. I'll see you around the office?'

'Probably not, actually. I've got meetings all day. Goodnight, Marina. Don't worry. I'm sure everything will be fine.'

Marina had no time to dwell on her problems once she arrived at work. There was so much to do, and full concentration was required. She was late leaving the office, so she called at the local takeaway for pizza. She was far too tired to cook anything tonight, takeaway would have to do. She wasn't looking forward to ringing Jon's parents, and she was worried about how her phone call to Roberto would go. She'd heard no more from him since the previous day.

When she got in, she put the washing machine on, quickly ate the pizza, and settled down with her mobile phone.

'Hello, Mrs Bentley. How's Jon?'

'He didn't look so good today. I think he was depressed by what the doctor said.'

'Oh, what was that?'

'The doctor warned him it could take quite a while for his memory to come back, and he might never remember some things.'

'That's awful.'

'It is. I feel so sorry for him. The doctor signed him off work for the next six weeks. He said it could take even longer to recuperate. Jon really broke down then. We didn't know how to pacify him,' Barbara sobbed.

'I'm so sorry.' Marina felt like crying too. She hadn't expected to hear such bad news. 'Did you speak to the doctor on his own?'

'Yes, Cecil and I had a word with him. He told us to be very careful about what we say. He said Jon's under enough pressure, without us adding to his stress by referring to things of which he has no recollection.'

'So you were right, persuading me to let him believe we were still together.'

'I was. Please don't tell him you're not.'

'I won't. I don't want to cause any more distress. I wish you had better news.'

'So do I. You will come to see him again soon?'

'Of course.' What else could she say? Poor Jon. She felt so upset for him. 'What will happen about his job in Australia?'

'He can't return there — not that he wants to at the moment — but when his memory comes back, he may be upset. His boss was very kind, quite sympathetic and understanding. The bank will keep a job open for him to go back to when he has recovered, but it will be in London.'

'It's good that they'll do that.'

'Yes, but I'm not sure how he will feel about working in London. His boss explained that they have more branches there, so it's easier to keep a job open. He also said there's no need for Jon to hurry back to work. He should be completely recovered before he attempts to return.'

'Not many bosses would take that attitude.'

'You're right. What worries me,

173

though, is if Jon's memory doesn't ever get back to normal, will he be able to work?'

'I'm sure he will, Barbara. We must be positive. Did the doctor say when he could go home?'

'Hopefully in a couple of weeks, which is good — although Jon doesn't think so. He wants to leave now. I'll get his room ready in a few days. I'm going home on Friday. Cecil will stay on in Edinburgh until he comes out of hospital. It's a good thing we're both retired, otherwise I don't know what we would have done.'

'The time will soon pass.'

'That's what I keep telling Jon. So, as soon as he does come home, will you visit him?'

'Yes, of course.'

'Thanks, Marina. It made such a difference to Jon, seeing you again. If he knows you will be coming soon, he will have something to strive for. I'll let you go now, but I'll keep in touch. He will probably ring you in a day or two.'

That was what Marina feared. She didn't want to be unkind, but conversations with Jon were going to be difficult, now he had declared his feelings for her. He'd never even hinted at anything like that before he'd gone to Australia.

After Marina had ended her conversation with Barbara, her next task was to ring Roberto. She felt nervous and shaky. What was she going to say to him? She was committed to visiting Jon again. How would Roberto take that? He hadn't listened to her before, so why would he now? Did she have to tell him? If she didn't, she would feel she was being sneaky, so she would try to explain things. After all, Roberto was a paramedic, and his father was a doctor, so he had probably come across cases like this before. Marina reminded herself that he had apologised. Maybe this time he would give her a chance to explain.

She made herself comfortable on the sofa, picked up her phone, and rang Roberto.

He answered immediately. 'Hello, Marina. How are you?'

'Very well, thank you. Rather tired, though. And you?'

'I feel guilty for upsetting you. I'm sorry for my behaviour before you went away. I don't know what came over me. Will you forgive me?'

'Yes, Roberto.'

'You will? That's good. I was afraid you wouldn't.'

'I think I can see your point of view. You must have thought I was letting you down to visit a former boyfriend. But the only reason I was doing that was because of the accident, and his mother begging for my help.'

'I've thought about that, and I can see I was being unreasonable.'

'Let's forget about it and start again.'

'A good idea. So, when can you see me?'

'When are you free?'

'Next Sunday. Would you like to go out somewhere?'

'That would be lovely.'

'If it's fine again, we could go to the coast.'

'I'd like that.'

'I'll pick you up at ten-thirty if that's okay? Can I ask, how was your friend?'

'Not too good.' Marina had been wondering when he would ask about Jon.

'You can tell me all about it on Sunday. I'll leave you in peace, now. You sound very tired.'

'I am. I can hardly keep my eyes open.'

'Sleep well, Marina, and make sure you wear sensible shoes on Sunday. We don't want any more accidents.'

He'd never let her forget that! She hung up feeling much happier, but also still slightly worried about what Roberto would say when she told him she'd agreed to see Jon again.

★   ★   ★

The next day, Marina returned to work. It was still extremely busy, and there was no time to speculate about Roberto, or anybody else.

During the course of the week, she bumped into her father a couple of times, but there was no opportunity for a prolonged chat.

'Everything all right?' he enquired, in passing.

Marina knew he was referring to her and Roberto.

'Yes, fine.'

'That's good,' he smiled. 'When are you seeing him again?'

'If you mean Roberto, next Sunday.'

'Have a good time.'

'I'll try to.'

★ ★ ★

On Wednesday, Marina received a call from Jon.

'It was lovely to see you at the weekend. Please come again soon.'

'I will, when you go back to your parent's house.'

'But that might not be for a long time.'

'Your mum told me a couple of weeks.'

'Now they're saying it could be longer.'

'Oh, Jon, why's that?'

'The wounds on my head are not healing as quickly as they thought, and they're still worried about my memory. I hate it in hospital. I'm so bored. I need to see you, Marina.'

This was bad news. She was upset for Jon, but there was nothing she could do about it.

'I really can't come to Scotland again at the moment. Apart from the time, I can't afford the expense.'

'I'll pay for you.'

'I couldn't accept that.'

'Why not? You are my girlfriend, and I hope, one day, you'll be more than that.'

How was she going to get out of this?

'I told you, Jon, we should wait until you're better before any decisions are made.'

'Yes, I do remember.' His voice was

sharp. 'I haven't forgotten everything, you know.'

'I know. I'm sorry, Jon. I will come as soon as you go back to your parents' house. That's all I can promise.'

'Oh, Marina, I'm so miserable. Life's not worth living, stuck in hospital. I can't cope with this.'

'You're not to say that. In a few weeks, you'll be back to normal.'

'Will I?'

'Of course you will.' Marina tried to sound convincing. She was beginning to wonder what the outcome would be. She knew that depression could impede his recovery. 'Your parents are visiting you frequently. You're not alone.'

'Yes, and I'm grateful for that, but, Marina, it's you I want to see. Can't you understand? You're the girl I want to marry.'

She was getting nowhere with Jon. She was out of her depth. 'Just concentrate on getting better, please, Jon. I'll ring in a few days, and I'll be thinking about you.'

That was true, at least.

'And you can text me whenever you like. I'll reply when I can.' Should she have said that? Probably not, but she was feeling so sorry for him.

'It's not easy to text, Marina. My fingers are still painful from the accident.'

'Oh, I didn't think.'

'That's all right. I know you're very busy, so I'll wait for you to ring me.'

★　★　★

On Friday, Marina was not so late home from work. She telephoned Barbara.

'Any more news?'

'I think Jon's beginning to come to terms with what's happened. Seeing you has helped. I've tried to explain that you can't keep coming to Scotland, and he seems to have accepted it.'

'That's good.'

'I've changed my plans, and will stay with him a bit longer. Cecil will go home instead, and sort through our post and do anything that's necessary. I'll let you know how things are in a few days. And thanks, Marina. For being so understanding. You didn't have to get involved. It's our problem, not yours.'

'I was very fond of Jon. We were together for over a year, remember. I couldn't just abandon him when he was in trouble.' Now she felt guilty. She hadn't done much.

'Yes, but that was in the past. Cecil and I have been discussing this. He's made me realise I was being unfair to you, continually talking about you two getting back together.'

'That's all right. You were just trying to help Jon.'

'I know he proposed to you,' Barbara continued, 'but we will do our best to convince him that decisions like that must wait until he has made a full recovery.'

'Thanks, Barbara.'

Marina hung up, feeling relieved that at last Barbara seemed to understand the situation. She then rang Jon, but it went immediately to voicemail.

'Hope you're doing well,' she said. 'I'll try again in a few days.'

She guessed that he was having treatment or the doctors were doing their rounds and he was unable to talk.

* * *

On Saturday, Marina took the opportunity of catching up on her housework. She made a brief telephone call to her father, who said, 'Sorry, can't stop now. Amelia's waiting for me. Going to the cinema. Is everything okay?'

'Yes. You enjoy yourself, Dad.'

At least she hadn't had to go into details about Jon.

During the evening, she received a text from Roberto.

Hello Marina, looking forward to seeing you tomorrow, if you are still coming out with me. Roberto.

Even now, he didn't trust her. Marina felt somewhat annoyed.

Why wouldn't I be coming? she texted back.

No reason. Sorry, came the reply.

In her mind, Marina imagined him saying, 'Are you sure you want to come out with me? Wouldn't you rather go out with your ex-boyfriend?'
Then she chided herself. She was misjudging Roberto, getting too cynical. She replied to his text.

See you in the morning.

Marina spent the rest of the evening wondering how they would get on, and what Roberto would say when she explained to him about Jon. Would it be a happy day, or would there be more problems on the horizon?

11

Marina was awakened early the next morning by the sound of birdsong and the sun streaming through the window. It was going to be another hot day. She quickly had a shower, put on a cool, cotton dress, and made some toast and a bowl of porridge.

As she was drinking a cup of tea, her mobile rang. She hoped it was Roberto, but it was Jon.

'Hello Marina. Thank you for your voicemail. Sorry I missed your call.'

'That's all right. How are you, Jon?'

'Not too good. I'd be better if you were here.'

Marina sighed, inwardly.

'I'm sorry, but I can't keep travelling to Edinburgh.'

'I know. I shouldn't have said that. I was having a chat with the consultant when you called. That's why I didn't answer my phone. I thought I'd better leave it until today to reply, in case you were busy, or having an early night.'

'Thanks for being so thoughtful.'

'I didn't wake you up, did I?'

'No, the birds did. I was just having my breakfast. What did the consultant have to say?'

'Not much. Just that I have to be patient, which isn't easy.'

'No, I suppose not.'

'I'm not a patient person. Anyway, it's a lovely day here. I woke up hours ago. I couldn't sleep. I was wondering what you were doing. Oh, Marina, I do wish you were here. I miss you so much. I know it wouldn't have been very exciting for you, but we could have gone out into the hospital grounds, just the two of us. Spent some time together.'

'It's lovely here too,' Marina replied. 'You can go out into the grounds with your mother when she visits.'

'I know that, but it's not the same. I want to be with you.'

'I've told you. I'll come when I can.'

'I know. Thanks Marina.'

'I haven't done much. You don't have to thank me.' She felt terrible, knowing she wasn't being completely honest with Jon. 'So, you're no better?' Marina changed the subject.

'Not really. I still can't remember much, and the pain in my head is still there.'

'Did you tell the consultant that?'

'Yes.'

'What did he say?'

'Keep taking the pills.'

'But they're not helping?'

'Actually, I've stopped taking them. I don't want to become dependent on them. I think they made my memory worse.'

'But if the doctor's told you to carry on with the pills, shouldn't you do as he says? That might be why you aren't feeling any better.'

'Maybe, but I'm so fed up with being treated like an invalid. I just want to get back to normal.'

'Yes, I can see that, but I really do think you should keep taking the pills.'

'Okay, I'll do it. To please you.'

'No, you must do it to help you get better.'

'Whatever you say, Marina. Anyway, that's enough about my condition. What are you doing today?'

'I don't know. Nothing much, probably.'

More lies! She couldn't tell Jon she was going out with Roberto.

'I'll be thinking of you, and wishing we were together,' Jon answered.

'You just concentrate on getting better.'

'I'll try. I'll let you finish your breakfast now. Goodbye, Marina. We'll talk again soon.'

'Yes Jon, I'd like that.' Another lie, she thought. They were coming too easily.

She looked at the clock. It was half past nine. She had an hour to get ready for Roberto.

At ten-thirty sharp, Roberto arrived. He eyed her up and down, and smiled broadly.

'Hello, Marina. I can see you took notice of what I said.'

'What do you mean?'

'Your shoes.' He pointed to them. 'You're wearing sensible trainers.'

'Well, I wouldn't want you having to rescue me again. Anyway, we're going to the coast, not a wedding. I'm not going to walk along the beach in three inch heels. I'm not that silly,' Marina said haughtily.

'Don't get all uppity. I'm only teasing,' Roberto answered. 'You look very nice. Dressed perfectly for our day beside the sea. Let's go.'

Marina picked up her bag and followed him to his car. As they drove along she realised she still didn't know how to take Roberto. She was never sure if he was being serious or not.

'Where are we going?' she asked.

'I thought Frinton might be good. It shouldn't take too long to get there, and it's a lovely day for strolling along the beach with your feet in the sea, if you like doing that sort of thing. I know a nice place to get Sunday lunch. How does that sound?'

'Perfect.'

'I'm glad it suits you.'

'Did your mother mind you missing Mass today?' Marina enquired.

'No. I don't go with her every week. She doesn't expect that. She knows I often have to work. I go when I can.'

'We could have set off a bit later, if you'd wanted to go with her.'

'No, that's all right Marina. I wanted to take you out for the day. Besides, I attended Mass yesterday evening. They have a service at six o'clock. I just had time to get there after I finished my shift. What about you Marina? Do you go to church?'

'Sometimes. Not as often as you. I used to, but I seem to have got out of the habit recently.'

'We'll have to remedy that situation,' Roberto said smiling. 'Maybe you could come with me and my mother one week? That is, if you have no objection to attending a Catholic Mass.'

'I'll think about it.'

When she'd been a child, her parents had sent her to a Baptist Sunday School, which she guessed would be very different from a Catholic service. Marina was wondering what her father would say if she did. She decided that if Roberto asked her again, she would go. She could do what she wanted, without having to seek her father's approval. He hadn't sought hers when he got involved with Amelia. Marina was also feeling pleased that Roberto was talking about the future.

For the rest of the journey, they chatted amicably and Marina felt quite relaxed. Nothing was said about her trip to see Jon the previous week, and she began to think that Roberto wasn't going to make any reference to it.

When they arrived at their destination, he bought two coffees from a stall on the sea front, and they found a seat nearby, where they sat drinking and admiring the view.

'Do you fancy having a paddle?' Roberto asked when they'd finished their drinks.

'I'd love one,' Marina replied.

They found the path leading down to the beach, took off their shoes, put them into their rucksacks, rolled up the bottoms of their trouser legs and picked their way across the sand and shingle to the water's edge.

Roberto stepped into the waves first.

'Come on Marina,' he called. 'It's lovely.'

She followed, but quickly ran back when she felt the chill of the water.

'It's not cold,' he yelled against the wind, which was whistling around them.

'It is for me,' she answered.

'Don't be such a chicken,' he shouted.

'I'm not,' she replied. She gingerly put her toes back into the water. She wasn't going to have him calling her that. Determinedly following behind Roberto, she continued walking along, ignoring the cold until she managed to catch up with him.

After a few minutes of paddling together, she looked around and noticed there were very few people on this stretch of the beach. She also observed that there was a bank of grey clouds heading their way.

'I think it's going to rain, Roberto.'

'Nonsense. It's a lovely day.'

'Look over there,' Marina said, pointing to the left.

'Oh. I hadn't spotted those. Maybe we'd better head back. I don't want you getting wet.'

'A bit of rain won't hurt me,' Marina protested, stepping once more between the waves.

'I think we should turn back though. We've quite a walk to the car, and if it really comes down we'll get soaked.'

'Okay.'

Marina tiptoed across the beach, following Roberto until they found the path leading to the road. They found a rock to sit on, quickly rubbed the sand from their feet and put on their trainers. As they were sitting there, they heard the rumble of thunder in the distance.

'We'd better hurry.' Roberto held out his hand to her. 'Come on, it's going to pour down in a minute. Hold onto me. I don't want you twisting your ankle again. It's probably still a bit weak from your accident, and it could easily give way.'

'Okay, Doctor.' Marina smiled, but took his hand, and they ran back to the car. He unlocked the door, pushed her inside and then clambered in himself, as there was a flash of lightning and a loud clap of thunder.

'We made it,' Roberto said breathlessly, as the rain came down in torrents.

'You were right. It's a good thing we

came back when we did,' Marina gasped.

'We'll sit here for a while and wait for the storm to pass over. Then we'll head for the restaurant and get some lunch.'

They peered through the windows, watching the few people who were still outside battling with their umbrellas, or trying to reach the shelter of their cars.

'That was unexpected,' Roberto remarked. 'I was sure it was going to be fine all day.'

'I never trust the weather forecast,' Marina replied. 'They're often wrong.'

'You're too cynical. Do you trust anyone?'

'Not many people, I suppose,' she smiled. That was true. She trusted her father, of course, but not Amelia. Not yet.

'What about me?' Roberto interrupted her train of thought.

'I don't know you very well, but I wouldn't have come out with you if I didn't trust you.'

'That was a very diplomatic answer,'

Roberto laughed, and she joined in. 'Let's head for the restaurant. It's not too far away. I'm starving. What about you?'

'I'm hungry, too.'

'Good.'

Twenty minutes later, they were seated in a smart restaurant, in a little alcove, partitioned with trellis and wrought iron, giving them privacy from the other diners.

'What a lovely place,' Marina remarked. 'This barn conversion's amazing.'

She gazed up at the triangular-shaped roof. It was flooded with light of different hues coming through huge, partially stained-glass windows.

'This is really spectacular.'

'It is, and the food's good too.'

'So you've been here before?'

'Yes, a few times.'

Marina wondered when, and with whom, but didn't ask.

They made their choices from the extensive menu, and settled back to enjoy their pre-lunch drinks.

'So, how was your trip to Scotland last weekend?' Roberto suddenly asked.

'Okay.'

'And your ex-boyfriend — how is he?' Roberto stared at her intently.

'He's not too good.'

'You said he was in an accident, a coach crash?'

'Yes, that's right. He had several injuries, but they are healing. His main problem though, is his head. It's all so complicated,' Marina sighed. 'Do you really want to hear about it?'

'Of course. Tell me.'

'Well, he's suffering from amnesia. His memory has been badly affected. He's forgotten everything that happened in the past few months. He has no recollection of the accident, and doesn't remember going on holiday to Scotland. And . . . and he thinks that we're still together.'

'Oh, I understand now. That's why you rushed off to see him.'

'His mother begged me to go, as he

kept asking to see me. He doesn't remember that we split up.'

'And you didn't want to upset him?'

'The doctors said we should be very careful, and not give him too many shocks.'

'That's right. If he becomes too distressed it will hinder his recovery. Oh, Marina, I'm so sorry. I should never have shouted at you on the phone. It was inexcusable. You were just trying to help him, and I was so nasty. I was jealous, Marina. I didn't give you a chance to explain.'

'No, you didn't, but I can see why you were so angry. Being stood up isn't pleasant, especially if it's for an ex-boyfriend. I can understand how it must have seemed to you.'

'You're being too kind, Marina. I don't deserve it.'

'Let's just forget it.'

The waiter arrived with their food, and nothing more was said about Jon until they'd finished eating and were sipping coffee.

'So, are you going to see Jon again?' Roberto asked.

'I'll have to. I can't get out of it. I hate all this deception, but I don't know what else I can do.'

'Do the doctors think his memory will improve?'

'Yes, eventually. Then he'll probably be horrified at all the things he's said to me since the accident.' Now why had she said that? Roberto was going to want to know what she meant, and she couldn't tell him that Jon had proposed.

'That sounds interesting.'

'I won't bore you with all the details.'

'Okay. I think we've spoken enough about Jon for today. But another time, I would like to know why you split up.'

'And you can tell me about your past romances.'

'That won't be very interesting.'

Marina thought it might be, especially if he told her about Amelia.

'Now, if you're finished,' Roberto continued, 'I'll drive us into Clacton.

It's still pouring, so maybe we can go to the cinema. There must be a film you'd like to see. It's far too wet to go back on the beach.'

'That's a good idea.'

★ ★ ★

The rest of their time together passed pleasantly, and they arrived back at Marina's flat just before midnight, both tired after their busy day. Marina was happy that everything had gone so well, despite the inclement weather.

Before saying goodnight, a date had been arranged for the middle of the week, when Roberto had finished work.

'Are you free on Wednesday evening?' he'd enquired. 'I'm on the early shift, so I should be home at about five, unless some major catastrophe occurs. I could drive over, pick you up and take you out for a drink, if you'd like?'

'Yes, I'd love to. Wednesday is good for me too; I actually have the afternoon off, as I've put in so many extra hours recently. I could meet you in London. That would save you having to drive over to me and back. I'd planned to go shopping in Oxford Street anyway, and I always go by train.'

'I don't mind driving. I do it on and off all day, so it comes as second nature to me. But if you're going to be in London, it makes sense to meet you there.'

'It's a pity you haven't got the day off too.'

'Even if I had, this week I have to spend all my free days working on my art, so I wouldn't have been able to see you anyway. There's a lot to do, and I don't want any distractions.'

'Gosh, are you sure you can spare the time to go out with me Wednesday evening?' Marina asked, sarcastically, feeling somewhat put out by Roberto's reply.

'Of course, or I wouldn't have asked. I don't mean to be awkward, but I really do need time on my own to catch up on my project.'

'Can I ask what it is?'

'I'll tell you when it's completed. Now I must go home, otherwise I'll never get up in the morning. I'll text to let you know where and when to meet.'

'Okay. Thank you, Roberto, for a lovely day.'

'I enjoyed it too,' he answered, bending down and gently kissing her cheek. 'Goodnight Marina.'

★　★　★

She was busy at work for the next couple of days, arriving home late and very tired. She had little time to dwell on what Roberto had said, or her day with him, or to anticipate their next meeting.

Jon telephoned again. He seemed to have made little progress. He still kept begging Marina to come to Edinburgh.

'I can't come at the moment. I'm far too busy to arrange that,' she told him, feeling guilty that, as before, she wasn't strictly telling the truth. Her conscience was pricking her once again.

★   ★   ★

After a successful shopping trip, Marina met Roberto on Wednesday evening. He took her to a cosy bar near St. Paul's Cathedral.

'I can see you've had a good time,' Roberto remarked, pointing to the plastic carrier bags she was clutching.

'Yes, I've got some real bargains today. There were sales everywhere.'

They settled down to look at the menu. Time seemed to pass very quickly, as they ate, drank and chatted.

Halfway through the evening, Marina went to the Ladies' Cloakroom to freshen up. As she washed her hands, she reflected on how well everything had gone. It seemed they'd both got over their initial difficulties in adjusting to each other. Roberto seemed to have mellowed, or maybe she had just got used to being with him.

As Marina came out of the cloak-room, she noticed there was a man standing in front of Roberto, talking to him. She had to wait for a while to walk back, as a woman was coming towards her, pushing a wheelchair.

'Sorry I can't go any faster,' the woman puffed.

'That's quite all right. You take your time. I'm not in a hurry.'

As Marina stood waiting, she could hear the conversation which was taking place between Roberto, who had his back to her, and the stranger.

'And how's Rhoda?' the man asked. 'Are you still with her?'

Marina strained to hear Roberto's reply.

'Yes,' he answered. 'Of course.'

'I thought so. I don't think you two will ever part ways.'

'No, you're probably right.'

12

Marina put her hand to her mouth. Roberto had a partner! He'd been deceiving her the whole time.

As soon as the woman with the wheelchair had manoeuvred past, Marina ran back into the ladies' cloakroom. She sank down onto the sofa, which was positioned in front of a large mirror. For a moment, she felt too stunned to react, but then the tears began to course down her cheeks. She was glad that she was the only person in there. Then, adrenalin kicked in and rage took over. The liar! The cheat! How could Roberto do this to her? What should she do?

Her first thought was to go and have it out with him, but that would cause a scene, and Marina hated the thought of that. She also knew that she was so furious, she might say or do something which she'd later regret. No. Instead she'd leave him sitting there, wondering where she was. That's what she'd do. She'd noticed there was a rear exit to the building, leading to a busy main road. She'd sneak out there. Roberto had his back to her, so he wouldn't see her leave.

Marina quickly used her mobile to call a cab, and was assured that someone would be there in five minutes. It wouldn't take long to get to the nearest railway station, and it shouldn't be too expensive. She was glad she'd taken quite a bit of cash out with her; she would have no problem paying for the taxi. She'd be home very late, but that couldn't be helped.

She stared at her reflection in the mirror. She felt sick, and her face was white. Why had Roberto done this to her? And what did he hope to gain from it?

She heard the door open, and a woman entered.

She saw Marina slumped on the sofa,

her knuckles white from clenching her fists so tightly. The woman came over to her. 'Are you all right?' she enquired.

'I'll be okay in a minute,' Marina replied, shakily. 'I just got a bit too hot. I needed to sit down for a minute.'

'Yes, it is very warm. You look rather pale. You're not going to faint, are you?'

'No. I'm feeling a bit better, now.' Marina tried to pull herself together. She sat up straight and took a deep breath.

'Are you with someone?'

'No.' Not any more, she thought. Roberto would have no idea why she hadn't returned. He might make a few guesses, but he wouldn't know it was because she'd heard what that stranger had said ... Roberto ... and Rhoda. That was her name.

The woman was gazing intently at Marina. 'Well, can I ring anyone for you? It's not nice being on your own when you feel ill.'

'It's all right, thank you. I've rung for

a taxi. They'll be here in a minute.'

'Would you like me to wait until they come?'

'No. I'll be fine, thanks.'

'Okay. I'll leave you in peace. My husband's probably wondering where I am. Goodbye, dear. Hope you'll soon be better.'

'I will. Thank you.'

The woman walked off and Marina stood up. She knew the woman was only trying to be helpful, but she was glad to be alone once more. She crept out of the door, observing that the woman was approaching Roberto, who was still in conversation with the stranger. She hurried to the rear door, and walked outside to the road, just as the taxi was arriving.

'Where to?' the driver enquired, as Marina climbed inside.

Before she could reply, she noticed Roberto, the stranger, and the woman from the cloakroom, all coming out of the back door towards them.

'Wait,' Roberto yelled.

'Just drive,' Marina ordered. 'Ignore him.'

'Okay. You can tell me where to go in a moment.' The taxi lurched forward. 'I guess you're trying to get away from those people.'

'That's right. Don't stop for them. Pull away as fast as you can, please.'

★ ★ ★

Two hours later, Marina was back at home, stretched out on her bed, clutching a box of tissues and trying to stem the tears, which were flowing freely down her face. She'd been completely taken in by him. It had never occurred to her that he might have a partner; he could even be married. She'd assumed he was free like herself.

Marina's landline and mobile phone had been ringing constantly, but she ignored them, assuming it was Roberto. She vowed never to speak to him again. And if it wasn't him, she was in no fit state to talk to anyone else. Of course, it might be Jon or his mother, she mused, but she couldn't possibly speak to them now. They would have to wait until later, when she'd got over this and felt better. Would that ever happen though? It had to. She wouldn't waste her life pining over someone who was so unscrupulous.

Finally, Marina decided to get into bed. She was exhausted from crying, and feeling these strong emotions. She'd never experienced this before. She kept asking herself why she'd got into such a state over Roberto. After all, she'd only met him a short time ago. Then she remembered her father's words: 'You'll know the moment you meet someone if he's the right man for you.'

She'd begun to think Roberto was the man for her, and had hoped he felt the same way; she'd been so mistaken. He was dishonest, and unworthy of her love. She'd never let any man deceive her in that way again. She'd be much more wary the next time — if there was a next time. Eventually, with these thoughts whirling around her head, she fell into a troubled sleep.

The next morning, Marina found it hard to get ready for work, but felt compelled to go in. She could have sent a message and said she was ill, but her conscience wouldn't let her. If she didn't go in, all her colleagues would be inconvenienced, and that wouldn't be fair on them.

She quickly got washed and dressed, applied some make-up to her pale face, drank a cup of tea and grabbed a breakfast biscuit, which she consumed as she made her way to work.

Everyone was busy in her office, and there was little time for conversation, for which Marina was grateful. She had to concentrate on the tasks in hand, and had no time to dwell on her problems.

She was very glad her mobile had stopped ringing. She guessed Roberto had given up. She didn't suppose she would hear from him again. He'd left several messages and texts, which she'd ignored.

That evening, after she'd forced herself to eat a small meal, Marina took delight in deleting all of Roberto's texts without looking at them. Then she turned to her landline. There were six messages. She would have to listen to them before they could be erased.

The first was from Roberto.

'You haven't answered my texts, so I'm trying your landline. I know you won't be home for a while, but I hope that by the time you get there you will have calmed down. What's going on, Marina? I couldn't believe it when I saw you getting into that taxi. Why did you run off? Had you planned this all the time? What am I supposed to have done? I guess you must think it's something bad, otherwise you wouldn't have left like that, but I am completely mystified. Please ring, and put me out of my misery.'

Marina quickly deleted the call, and proceeded to listen to the next one, which was from Jon, as was the third, all sent the previous evening. Then there were two others from Jon, which had come while she was at work. They all said much the same thing: he was missing her, and when was she coming to see him?

The final message was from Roberto. He'd sent it earlier that evening.

'As you have ignored all my calls and texts, I guess we're over. I still have no idea why. I must say, I'm shocked by your behaviour. I would have expected that if you wanted to finish with me, you would have had the decency to tell me to my face.' His tone was clipped and she could tell he was trying to conceal his anger. 'I won't say it was nice knowing you. It's only caused me anguish. I don't suppose we will ever meet again, which is probably for the best. So, goodbye, Marina.'

She burst into floods of tears as she heard those words. She alternated between despair and anger. He was being so unfair. Roberto was acting as if she was in the wrong, but he was the one causing all the misery.

After a while, she calmed down, deciding that she was better off without him. She'd put him out of her mind, and concentrate on helping Jon recover. She went into the bathroom and had a shower, all the time telling herself she was washing Roberto out of her system.

She made some coffee and sat planning what to do. Now Roberto was no longer around, there was no reason why she couldn't visit Jon. She'd go a week on Friday, in the evening, and stay two nights. Then her conscience kicked in. Was it fair to lead Jon on, just because things were finished with Roberto? Well, she wasn't exactly leading him on, she told herself. She was helping him, really. After all, she didn't want to do or say anything that could impede his progress.

What if Jon proposed again, though? What would she do then? She'd have to tell him once again that it was too soon to make any plans for the future.

Marina decided to see if there were any flights available before replying to Jon's messages. She didn't want to raise his hopes and then have to disappoint him because she couldn't get a flight. She looked online and found two suitable ones at the right time and price, so she booked them immediately and then telephoned Jon's mother.

'He'll be so pleased,' Barbara answered. 'He keeps asking when you are coming. I'll get you a room in my hotel again, if you would like that?'

'Yes please, that would be very kind. How is Jon?'

'No change, I'm afraid. We were all hoping his memory would have come back by now.'

'Have the doctors said anything?'

'No, they're very non-committal. They say it could return soon, or it could be much longer. No one knows.'

'How is Jon taking it?'

'He's very down. He still has pain in his head, and he feels so weak.'

'But that will pass?'

'Yes, but progress seems to be very slow, and Jon is not the most patient of people. I think his mental state is hindering his progress. But seeing you might be the tonic he needs. I know it's hard, Marina, but I think you are the key to Jon's recovery.'

'Please don't say that Barbara.' Marina didn't want that responsibility.

'But it's true. He was more like his old self when you were there that weekend. Have you told him yet that you're coming?'

'No. I wanted to speak to you first.'

'I'm sure just knowing he'll see you soon will make a big difference.'

'Okay. I will ring him now.'

'Thanks, Marina,' Barbara answered. 'I'll book you into my hotel, and I'll see you a week on Friday.'

Marina put down the receiver, made another drink and braced herself for the phone call.

Jon answered immediately. 'Hello, Marina. I've missed you so much. I've been trying to contact you the last couple of days, but I guess you must have been busy.'

'Yes, it's been frantic at work, and I was home too late to ring.' More lies, she thought. 'How are you?'

'Much better for hearing your voice. Have you missed me?'

'I've some good news for you,' she replied, sidestepping his question.

'I need some. The doctors haven't given me much.'

'I've booked a flight to Edinburgh for Friday week, after work, and will stay for two nights this time.'

'That's wonderful news. I can't wait to see you. I feel better already.'

'Well, you'll have to wait until then,' she smiled. At least someone wanted her, she thought.

★   ★   ★

The next day, when Marina returned from work, she found another voicemail on her phone from Roberto. She hadn't expected this. He'd implied he wasn't going to contact her again. Her curiosity overcame her, and she listened to the message.

'I'm sorry for what I said the other day. I sometimes speak without thinking things through. But I really cannot understand why you're behaving this way. I genuinely have no idea what I'm supposed to have done. Please, Marina, at least tell me what's going on. That's only fair. Can we meet on Friday week? We need to talk. I'm doing a double shift next week to cover for someone who's off sick, so I'm not free until then.'

Surely he must realise why she was so angry. He couldn't possibly think she was the kind of girl who would go out with someone who was married or had a partner. Anyway, it was beside the point, as she couldn't see him that day anyway — she was off to Edinburgh. But doubts began to creep in. Should she have given him a chance to explain? Had she acted too hastily? She was in a quandary. Marina was curious about what Roberto had to say, but was still sure there could be no good explanation for it. She found herself wavering. Should she call him back?

Before she could make any decision, her landline phone rang. Marina picked up the receiver at once. It was her father. She hadn't heard from him for several days, for which she's been grateful. She knew he would ask about Roberto, and she hadn't wanted to lose control and burst into tears when his name was mentioned. She hoped that now, she would be more composed and able to handle his questions.

As predicted, it wasn't long before her dad said, 'When are you seeing Roberto again?'

'I'm not,' Marina blurted. 'We're finished.'

'Whatever's happened this time?'

'I don't want to discuss it.'

'What's he done? Perhaps I can help.'

'No one can.'

'You never know, I might. You can tell me; I'm your father.'

Marina knew her dad would persist in trying to find out what had happened. He meant well really, and only wanted the best for her, so finally she muttered, 'He's married.'

'No,' he gasped. 'I'm sure he's not.'

'Well, he's got a partner, then.'

'I don't believe it. I'm sure Amelia would have told me if that was the case.'

'I overheard him talking to some man, Dad. He said he was still with Rhoda and they would never part.'

'Are you quite certain that was what was said?'

'Yes. I'm not deaf.'

'There must be some misunderstanding.'

'I know what I heard.'

'I'll have a word with Amelia. Perhaps she will be able to shed some light on the situation. Rhoda, you say the name was?'

'Yes, but I don't want you talking to Amelia about it. Please don't tell her.'

'Why ever not?'

Marina knew it was irrational, but she didn't want Amelia to know what had happened. In her mind, she could imagine her gloating over it. Although Marina had no proof, she still felt convinced that Amelia and Roberto had been involved with each other at some point. Maybe Rhoda had come between them. It could even be that Amelia knew Roberto was with Rhoda, and that was why she hadn't look pleased when she heard that Marina was going out with him. Marina didn't know what to think.

'So, can I tell her? Marina? Are you still there?' Lionel was asking.

'Yes, I'm still here. I was just thinking.'

'Can I ask Amelia?' Lionel repeated.

'I suppose so,' Marina replied. At least she might get some answers. It wouldn't make any difference though. She was finished with Roberto.

'Good. I'll do that.'

'I'm off to see Jon again next Friday,' Marina said, changing the subject.

'Is that wise?'

'What do you mean?'

'You've just told me you have finished with Roberto, and now you're going to see Jon again. Don't do anything rash.'

'Of course I won't.' Marina was indignant.

'You're on the rebound from Roberto. You might get carried away, and do something you'll regret later.'

'I'm twenty-five, Dad. I'm not a child. You don't need to tell me how to behave.'

'I'm not trying to upset you. Just be careful. That's all. Look, I have to go now, Amelia's calling me. Goodnight, Marina.'

She hung up, feeling irritated, both with herself, and with her father for treating her like a child, suggesting she would act rashly. That wasn't her way — was it? Had she been too hasty in condemning Roberto, and not giving him a chance to explain? If he rang again, should she listen to what he had to say?

Marina was just about to get ready for bed, when she heard the telephone ringing. She answered immediately.

It was her father.

'Hello, Marina. I thought I should ring before you went to bed. I can clear up one important matter for you.'

'What's that?'

'I know who Rhoda is. Amelia's just told me.'

13

As Marina lay in bed that night, she tossed and turned in anguish at her foolishness. She'd jumped to the worst possible conclusions about Roberto, and now she'd found out that she'd completely misjudged him. She had no reason to doubt her dad's word. He'd assured her that Amelia knew Rhoda well, and could confirm that she was definitely not Roberto's wife. In fact, she was years older than him and very happily married to someone else.

'So what did the conversation I heard mean?' Marina asked.

'Rhoda is his agent. She sets up viewings of his paintings. She has been doing that for years. She likes to champion new artists. So you've made a real mess of everything. You should ring Roberto and apologise,' Lionel advised. 'If you explain what happened,

I'm sure he will understand.'

'I don't think he will. I feel awful. I never gave him a chance. I just thought the worst.'

She'd never imagined that Rhoda might be a business partner.

'Ring him up, Marina,' Lionel urged again. 'You've nothing to lose, and everything to gain.'

'I'm not sure I'm brave enough. Anyway, he'd probably hang up on me.'

'Well try it, and see what happens.'

'What I did was unforgivable.'

'No, it was just a silly misunderstanding. Not surprising really, given what you heard.'

'Yes, but I shouldn't have been listening in to his conversation.'

'You couldn't help overhearing.'

'I should have realised there was some other explanation, and not jumped to the wrong conclusion. I reacted so badly. I believed the worst of him, when there was no valid reason for doing so.'

'Ring Roberto, and tell him all this.'

'I don't think I dare.'

'That's not like you, Marina. You've never been lacking in courage.'

'Look, Dad,' she'd said, 'I don't want to discuss this anymore. It's late and I need to get to bed.'

'Okay, but remember what I've said. If you don't sort this out with Roberto, you'll regret it. And you'll be punishing yourself, as well as him.'

That was true, Marina thought. Her father had hung up then, and she'd got herself ready for bed, knowing that sleep would elude her.

She lay there full of remorse. She'd acted on impulse and it had got her into trouble. She could understand if Roberto wouldn't forgive her. She deserved his condemnation. She should have confronted him at the time, and not slunk off into the night. Then all this misery could have been avoided. Did she have enough courage to ring him, and if so, would he accept her apology?

Now, Marina regretted not reading

Roberto's messages. What had he said? She'd deleted them all. Would he do the same to her if she contacted him? And if she did try, should it be before her trip to Edinburgh, or would it be better to let things cool down and then ring him when she returned? Maybe it would be best to leave it for a few days, she decided. If, by some miracle, Roberto accepted her apology and then found out that she was going to visit Jon again, that could cause more trouble.

What if he rang her again? She'd have to reply, now she knew the truth. She couldn't ignore him.

Throughout the night, Marina mulled over these thoughts without coming to any conclusion, finally drifting off to sleep just before dawn.

The next day she was still in a quandary about what to do. Her father rang again in the evening.

'Have you phoned Roberto?'

'No.'

'Why not, you silly girl? I know you

really like him. Why are you punishing yourself?'

'I don't know what to say.'

'Just say you're sorry. I'm sure he'll understand.'

'I wish I could believe that.'

'Try it and see. Go on. You've got nothing to lose.'

That was true. After promising she would try to pluck up courage, Lionel hung up. It was some days before she would be visiting Jon. If she left phoning Roberto until after that, he really would think that she wanted nothing more to do with him. Maybe her father was right. She should be bold, and ring Roberto now. She picked up her mobile phone and rang his number. It immediately went to voice-mail. Oh no! Now what should she say?

'Roberto, it's Marina. I just wanted to say I'm sorry. I got the wrong idea about something, completely. I'm so sorry. I don't know what else to say. If you could give me another chance, I'll try to explain it to you.'

Now it was up to him. Would he ring her back? It was just her luck that he wasn't there when she rang. Then suddenly, she remembered he'd said he wasn't free until the day she was going to Edinburgh. He'd wanted to see her that day. She'd have to ring him back and tell him she couldn't see him that weekend. Once again, she picked up her phone, her hand trembling.

'Roberto, it's Marina again. I just thought I'd better tell you — in case you're interested — that I'm not available the Friday you suggested meeting. I have a prior engagement. In fact the whole weekend is booked up. But I will be free any day after that.'

She'd done it, so now it was up to Roberto to make the next move.

There were no phone calls from him during the next few days. Marina resigned herself to the fact that he would never forgive her for what she'd done, and there'd be no reconciliation. Her attempt had failed, and there was no one to blame but herself. It had been her last chance.

Lionel telephoned the night before her trip to Edinburgh, and was surprised to hear that Roberto hadn't replied to her messages.

'He'll get in touch, I'm sure. He's probably just very busy,' he tried to reassure her.

'Dad, I've got to accept that it's all over between us. There's nothing I can do about it.'

'I think you're being pessimistic.'

'No, I'm being realistic. Anyway, I must finish packing now, so I'll talk to you when I get back from Edinburgh.'

⋆　⋆　⋆

On Friday, after work, Marina set off for Scotland. Mrs Bentley met her at the airport and took her straight to the hotel. She quickly changed her clothes, and grabbed a bite to eat from the bar. It was too late to visit Jon that night, so Marina planned on having an early night to prepare for the next day.

'How's Jon?' she enquired.

'Very excited. Can't wait to see you.'

'What about his memory?'

'No change there. But maybe seeing you again will help.'

'I hope so,' Marina had replied. 'That's why I'm here. I want to be of some use.'

'Ring Jon up tonight,' Mrs Bentley urged.

'I will, later on.'

'Don't make it too late. They get the patients ready for bed quite early at that hospital.'

'Ok. I'll do it soon,' Marina promised.

They made arrangements for the next day. Barbara agreed that Marina should visit on her own in the morning, and they would go back together in the afternoon.

'That will give you and Jon a chance to talk, without us sitting there, listening,' Barbara said.

Marina decided to phone Jon before she had a shower.

'It's so nice to hear your voice again,' he told her. 'I've missed you so much. Have you missed me?'

Marina wished he wouldn't ask that question.

'Yes, of course,' she mumbled, trying to sound sincere. She didn't like telling lies, but she couldn't tell the truth: that she hadn't missed him at all. 'I'll be over as early as I can in the morning. I hope you have a good night's sleep.'

'I shall now I've heard your voice. Goodnight, my darling.'

Oh Jon, I'm not your darling, Marina wanted to say — but she knew she couldn't. She hated all this subterfuge.

Marina was in the process of having a shower when she heard her mobile phone ringing. She guessed it was Jon again.

Ten minutes later, she picked it up and saw that it was not Jon who had rung, but Roberto. Her heart nearly missed a beat. Why hadn't she got out of the shower and answered it? She hadn't been expecting to hear from him, not now. She groaned. She turned to her voicemail, and listened.

'Hello, Marina. This is Roberto. I really didn't think I would hear from you again. You ignored all my messages.' He paused. He sounded so cold and formal. 'Then suddenly, when I was resigned to the fact that everything was over between us,' Roberto continued, 'you rang to apologise for getting the wrong idea. About what? I'm completely baffled. You say you want a chance to explain, so, reluctant as I am to cause myself more pain, I think I do deserve an explanation. I suggest we meet next Tuesday evening. I'll come round to you when I finish my shift. It won't be before eight-thirty though. I hope I won't regret this. I'll see you then, unless I hear otherwise from you.'

Marina wondered whether she should ring him back, but courage failed her. She knew she'd be so nervous when he started talking in that pompous way, that she'd be unable to converse normally. He would probably ask why she couldn't see him this weekend, and she didn't want to have to tell him she was in Scotland, visiting Jon again. Roberto probably wouldn't be as understanding about it as he had been before. It might be better to just text him.

She did so when she was ready to go to bed. Her brief message read:

Thank you for getting in touch, Roberto. I am really sorry for what I did, and will try to explain why I behaved in that way. Looking forward to seeing you on Tuesday evening. Marina.

* * *

After another sleepless night, Marina set out to visit Jon. As soon as she walked into the ward, she could see that he looked much better than he had before. His bandages were gone, and he was sitting beside the bed, waving enthusiastically, a wide smile on his face.

'Marina, darling, it's wonderful to see you.' He reached out towards her and she let him kiss her on the cheek.

'Lovely to see you too,' she murmured, feeling guilty yet again for not being truthful. 'How are you, Jon?'

'So much better for seeing you.'

'You look it.'

'Yes, I don't think I'm quite so ugly now. My scars will fade, the doctors tell me, and then I'll be as good as new . . . Well, nearly,' he smiled.

They sat discussing the hospital routine, and Jon showed Marina how well he was progressing with walking. She held his arm as they promenaded around the ward.

'Knowing I was going to see you has helped. I've got something to aim for now.'

Why did he have to say stuff like that? She felt terrible again. This deception would have to stop. But how?

'What about your memory?'

'No change there, I'm afraid. I don't think it will ever come back completely. I'm resigned to that now. But it really doesn't matter. As long as we're together, that's the main thing.'

'But Jon, your memories are important. You need to know what you were doing, and how you were feeling, before you had the accident.' She had to make him realise this. He sounded too content with the way things were.

'Why?'

'Because things might not be ... quite as you think.'

'What does that mean?'

'Well, you weren't living in England, for a start. You had a new life, in Australia. There might be people you should contact, things you need to do ...'

'Don't you worry about that, Marina. My mother's been in touch with everyone in Australia who needs to know. I'm not going back there. My life is here now, with you. I have no idea why I went there. My boss has said they will keep a job open for me in England, so I don't have to go back to Australia.'

'That's good, about the job.'

'Yes. I just hope I will be able to cope with working again.'

'I'm sure it will all come back to you.'

'I hope you're right. I've no recollection of what I was doing.'

'Have the doctors said any more?'

'No. They won't commit themselves.'

'I'm sorry.'

'Marina, there's one thing I want to know.'

'What's that?'

'Why did I go to Australia and leave you behind?'

This was the one question Marina had been dreading. How could she answer without telling Jon the truth — that they were no longer together?

14

'Why did I go to Australia and leave you behind?' Jon repeated.

'Well . . . ' Marina paused, trying to think up a plausible answer. 'I didn't want to go. It was too far away from home. I didn't want to leave my Dad.' That part was true at least, she reflected.

'So why did I still go there, knowing you weren't happy about it?'

'It was something you really wanted to do. I wasn't going to stop you.'

He stared at her. 'But I don't understand why . . . '

Before Jon could continue, his mother walked in.

'Hello you two. I hope you've had a good morning. I think Jon has. I can see that by his face. He looks so much better.'

'I'm all the better for seeing Marina

again,' he smiled at her. 'I'm just trying to puzzle something out, though.'

Barbara looked from Jon to Marina, and quickly changed the subject.

'I expect they'll be bringing your lunch along soon. I've had some, so I guess you're probably ready for yours, Marina. You go and get yourself something. I'll keep Jon company for a while.'

Marina jumped up. 'Yes, I am rather hungry.'

Barbara had come along just in time, Marina thought, as she made her escape. It had saved her from trying to answer a tricky question. What reply could she have given, without explaining that she and Jon were no longer together? She would have had to tell him, even though the doctors had told them they shouldn't upset Jon. Sooner or later, though, he was going to have to be told, whatever the consequences. She couldn't continually live a lie.

An hour or so later, Marina returned

to the ward, and the three of them sat chatting for a while. Then, they took Jon for a walk along the corridor, so he could look through the windows at the attractive hospital gardens. Marina was glad that Barbara was there, so she wasn't on her own with Jon. She was worried that he might start quizzing her again.

The rest of the day passed uneventfully. Marina was relieved that Jon asked no more awkward questions. After they had left him at the hospital and were returning to their hotel, Marina told Barbara what Jon had said about Australia.

'I guessed that he'd been asking something like that. When I came into the ward and saw you together, he had a look of bewilderment on his face,' she answered.

'I'm going to have to tell him soon,' Marina replied.

'Are you quite sure there's no chance of you getting back together? It's just what he needs.'

'Barbara, that is not going to happen.'

'I'm sure his scars will fade. They have already. And it's only past memories that have gone. It won't affect him living a normal life.'

'That's not what's worrying me. I don't love him, Barbara.' She had to be clear. 'I can't pretend to be in love with him. Besides, after he went to Australia, I had no inkling that he saw me as anything other than a friend. When his memory returns, he'll probably feel the same way. I'm going to have to tell him. I can't keep up this pretence. It's no good for either of us.'

'Please don't do it, Marina. He might have a relapse.'

'It's a risk I will have to take. I'm sorry, Barbara. I've tried to avoid telling him, but I know he's going to ask me about Australia again. I've got to stop pretending.'

'Oh Marina, he'll be heartbroken.' Barbara's eyes filled with tears. 'My poor boy.'

'He's a grown man, not a boy.' Marina was becoming exasperated. 'He'll get over it.'

'What if he doesn't?'

'What's the alternative — I pretend for the rest of my life?'

They arrived back at the hotel, took the escalator up to their floor, and stood talking outside Marina's room.

'My mind's made up,' she said. The time had come to be decisive. 'I'm going to tell Jon tomorrow. I'd like to see him on my own. Shall I go in the morning?'

'I suppose so. I guess that nothing I say will make you change your mind.' Barbara sniffed. 'I'll go along in the afternoon, and do my best to console him.'

'It may not come to that. He may take it better than we think.'

'I hope so.'

* * *

The next morning, Marina had just got out of bed and was getting ready to go to the hospital when her mobile rang. It was Barbara.

'Oh Marina, I'm sorry to disturb you so early, but I've bad news.' Her voice broke as she tried to stifle a sob.

'What's happened?' Marina could feel her heart thumping.

'It's Jon. He's fallen over.'

'Oh no. Is he hurt?'

'He knocked himself out. He's unconscious.'

'How did it happen?'

'I don't know. I'm going to the hospital now.'

'I'll come too.'

'Thanks, Marina.'

'I'll be about fifteen minutes.'

'Okay. I'll meet you down in Reception. Then we can go together. I'll be glad of your company. I've phoned Cecil. He wanted to know if he should come up to Edinburgh, but I've told him to wait. I'll let him know later how Jon is.'

★ ★ ★

When they arrived at the hospital, they went straight to the ward, where they could see Jon lying down in bed. His face was white, and his head bandaged.

'Oh, my poor boy,' Barbara sobbed. 'What have you done?'

The nurse came over to them and put her arm around Barbara.

'Don't worry. He'll be all right. It looks worse than it is. Where his previous wounds were healing, the knock on his head has opened up the scar. It will heal, but he'll have a black eye and some bad bruises for a while. We've given him a scan and there's no permanent damage, luckily.'

'And his memory?'

'We don't know what effect this fall will have on that. We've given him a sedative. He needs plenty of rest, so he probably won't wake up for several hours.'

'How did it happen?' Marina asked.

'He got out of bed on his own and was walking across the ward when he tripped. He should have asked for help, but I think he wanted to be independent. He fell down and hit his head on the side of a bed. It knocked him out.'

The nurse turned to Marina. 'He'd been telling me earlier that his girl-friend was coming to see him, and he wanted to look his best for her. I understand it's upsetting for you that this has happened, but he will recover.'

'I hope you're right,' Barbara murmured.

'Try not to worry too much. It won't do Jon any good if he sees you upset. If there's anything else you want to know, I'll arrange for the doctor to have a chat with you.'

'Thank you very much,' Marina answered.

'You're welcome to sit with him, but he won't know you're there, and I doubt if he will wake up before tomorrow. The rest will do him good, help his brain recover from the trauma.'

Barbara and Marina sat beside Jon's bed for a while, watching him, but both realised that nothing was going to change that day.

Finally, Barbara said, 'There's not much point in you staying any longer. I think I will go back to the hotel and ring Cecil. I might call in again tonight, to see how he is. The nurse seemed quite certain that he'd get better, didn't she?'

'Yes, and she said the rest would do him good,' Marina assured Barbara. 'So you might as well have a break yourself.'

'I need one. All this hanging around hospitals is wearing me out. What will you do, Marina?'

'I'll probably go into the city. Have a look round Edinburgh before it's time to get my flight.'

'I'm sorry this had to happen when you were here,' Barbara sighed. 'Jon was so looking forward to being with you again, and now it's all been cut short. The trouble with him is, he's too impatient. He wanted to get over the accident in a few days, but it takes time.'

'Will you let me know how he is as soon as you have some news?'

'Of course. When will you come again?'

'I really don't know, Barbara.'

'What about next weekend? If you're worried about the cost, I'll pay for your flight. It will mean so much to Jon seeing you again.'

'I've got other arrangements for next weekend.' She hadn't, but she couldn't stomach the thought of coming back. Barbara didn't seem able to accept that there was no future for her and Jon. Marina supposed it was natural for a mother to stick up for her son's interests, but Barbara seemed to be taking it to extremes.

*   *   *

When Marina arrived home, she made a telephone call to her father, explaining what had happened.

'Oh dear,' he exclaimed. 'The poor fellow. What bad luck! Are you going back to see him when he comes round?'

'His mother wants me to, but I don't know. I feel sorry for Jon, but he still has the wrong idea about us. If I see him, I can't just carry on pretending. I'll have to tell him.'

'Maybe you should never have pretended in the first place.'

'I didn't really want to, but Barbara sort of strong-armed me into it.'

'You do get yourself into some scrapes. Have you heard from Roberto?'

'Yes.'

'And?'

'He's coming round on Tuesday evening.'

'Good. I told you he'd reply. Now, don't you go and mess things up again.'

'I'll try not to.'

'Be careful what you say about Jon. He might not understand.'

'I will. How's Amelia?' Marina changed the subject.

'Hasn't been too well the last few days. Think she's caught a virus.'

'I'm sorry. Wish her well for me.'

'I will, and I'll ring you on Wednesday to find out how you got on with Roberto.'

★ ★ ★

On Monday evening, Barbara rang Marina.

'I've some good news. Jon's woken up.'

'That's brilliant. How does he seem?'

'Not too bad, considering what's happened. They've had to give him a lot of pain relief for his head, but the good thing is, a few memories seem to have come back. It's almost as if the blow to his head has triggered something in his brain.'

'Oh, that's marvellous. Has he . . . said anything about me?'

'Yes. He wants to talk to you. Can you ring him tonight?'

'I'll do it soon. Thanks for letting me know, Barbara.'

'That's okay. Hope to see you again

soon. Bye, Marina.'

Marina wondered what Jon wanted to talk about. Would it be good news for her, or bad? Was he going to propose again, or had he remembered that they'd split up? As she was pondering these things, her mobile phone sounded. Thinking it would be a text from Jon, she picked it up, glanced at it, and saw that it was from Roberto.

Hope it's still okay to come over tomorrow evening. See you then. Roberto.

Marina replied, *Looking forward to it.*

It was true, she was looking forward to seeing him again — but she was also dreading it. Supposing he didn't accept her apology, and everything went wrong again between them? This was their final chance of sorting things out. Marina knew that if it didn't work this time, that would be the end.

First of all though, she had to phone Jon.

15

'Hello Jon. How are you?' Marina waited for his answer with baited breath.

'I'm okay, but I feel rather embarrassed.'

What was he going to say? Had he remembered that they'd split up and was embarrassed about his proposal?

'Why's that?' she asked.

'Well, it was such a silly thing to do, falling over like that. And it meant I missed a whole day of seeing you.'

'You couldn't help it.'

'I should have been more careful, but I'm so tired of being dependent on other people. I wanted to do things for myself.'

'You will in time. Your mum says your memory is getting better. Is that right?'

'I am beginning to remember a bit more.'

'That's good. Anything in particular?'

'I vaguely remember being in the coach, and there was this car coming towards us. And I remember being in a room with gold wallpaper. I think it must have been the hotel where I'd been staying in Edinburgh.'

'Have you told your mum? She would know what that room was like. She had to collect your things from the hotel.'

'I'll tell her when I see her. It's as if I'm looking through a fog. Everything seems misty. I think the sedatives the doctor gave me haven't helped.'

'You needed them, the nurse said, to allow your body to rest. It's a start though, you remembering about the hotel. Anything else?'

'I'm not sure. I don't want to talk about it just now. I'm so confused.'

'That's all right.' Marina didn't want to upset him.

'When can you come to Scotland again?'

'I don't know.'

'Make it soon, please, Marina.'

Now what could she answer? This was not the time to tell him the truth. She'd have to wait. Maybe with a bit of luck, she wouldn't have to. If his memory was beginning to come back, he might remember about Australia and them splitting up. She'd have to be patient.

'I'll try. You sound tired. I'll let you rest. Goodnight, Jon.'

'You're right. I do need to get some sleep. Thank you for ringing, Marina.'

★ ★ ★

The next evening, Marina hurried home from work, quickly made herself a meal, had a shower and changed into a pretty, pink summer dress. She was sitting down, attempting to read the newspaper, when Roberto arrived punctually at eight-thirty. She was excited, worried and nervous, all at the same time. What would be the outcome of the evening? How would

Roberto act? Would he accept her explanation? Or was this going to be their final meeting?

As she opened the door and saw Roberto standing there, looking incredibly handsome in his dark trousers and open-necked shirt, she felt overwhelmed and could feel her heart fluttering and her face becoming redder.

'Roberto. Come in, and sit down.'

'Thank you for seeing me. I wanted to hear what you had to say,' he said formally, his face inscrutable.

He followed Marina into the lounge and perched on the edge of an armchair. She sat down opposite him.

'Would you like a drink?' she asked.

'A black coffee would be lovely.'

'I'll go and make it. I won't be long.' Marina dashed off to the kitchen, glad to escape for a few moments, as Roberto settled himself down into the armchair, picked up a newspaper and started perusing it.

Marina quickly made the coffee,

placed the cups on a tray, took a deep breath and walked back into the lounge. The next few minutes would determine whether she and Roberto had any chance of a future together. She put the drinks on the table and sat down facing him.

He picked up his cup, took a sip and looked expectantly at Marina.

'You have something to say?'

'Yes,' she stammered. 'I'm sorry for running off and leaving you that day. It was unforgivable.'

'Oh, so you realise that now? And ignoring all my phone calls and texts, that was unforgivable too. Why did you do it?' he asked, harshly.

'I jumped to the wrong conclusion.'

'About what?'

'I overheard something.'

'And?'

'I misunderstood.'

'What did you hear? I am completely mystified by all this.'

'You remember I'd gone to the Ladies' cloakroom?'

'How could I forget?' Roberto answered. 'That's when you ran off like a frightened rabbit.'

'When I came out,' Marina continued, 'there was a lady pushing a wheelchair, and I couldn't get past very well, so I waited. I saw you talking to a man. You couldn't see me, you had your back to me.' She paused.

'Go on,' Roberto said, impatiently.

'I heard him ask if you and Rhoda were still together.'

'Yes. I remember that conversation. I didn't know you had heard it.'

'I couldn't help overhearing. I thought that . . . ' Her voice trailed away.

Roberto jerked up, spilling his coffee on the table. He glared at her. 'You thought that . . . what? Go on, say it, Marina.'

'I thought that Rhoda was your wife,' she whispered.

'My wife! You trusted me so little that you were ready to believe the worst without finding out the facts? You thought I was a married man, just having a fling with you? Was that it? I can't understand you, Marina.' He slammed his cup down on the table and slumped back into the chair.

'I'm sorry, Roberto. You're right. What more can I say? I know I shouldn't have run off like that. I should have come over and talked to you, found out the facts.'

'Yes, and not jumped to the wrong conclusion.'

'I know,' Marina whispered, close to tears.

'If you trust me so little, there's no hope for us.'

'I'm so sorry.' This was worse than she had feared. Roberto was looking at her with such scorn in his eyes.

'Maybe you will be better off with your wounded boyfriend,' he said bitterly. 'I suppose you've been to see him again. Was that why you couldn't see me on Friday?' He glared at Marina. 'Well? Did you go to see him?'

She couldn't lie to Roberto. 'Yes.'

'I knew it,' he fumed. 'He comes first, every time. Why am I bothering with you? It's all so pointless.'

'Let me finish,' she begged.

'Why should I? You accuse me of two-timing you, when all along, you've been carrying on with your ex-boyfriend.'

'How dare you say that?' Marina was furious. She'd been upset at first, but now rage was taking over at the injustice of his accusations. She stood up and faced Roberto, her eyes blazing with indignation. 'I only went to see Jon because I was trying to help him regain his memory after his accident. I explained all that to you, and I've apologised for what I did. There's nothing more I can do if you're determined to think the worst of me.' She sank down onto the chair, feeling hopeless and deflated. They were getting nowhere.

'Isn't that what you thought about me?' Roberto was gazing at Marina intently.

'Yes,' she murmured.

'Then,' he said, as his expression softened, 'we're both as bad as each other?'

'I suppose so.'

'In that case, why don't we put all this behind us and start all over again?' Roberto looked at her anxiously. 'What's your answer Marina?'

Had she misheard him? Roberto wanted to start all over again. Isn't that what she wanted?

'Well?'

'Oh, yes — please.'

Roberto leapt from his chair, rushed across the room and pulled Marina up. He put his arms around her, gazed into her eyes and whispered, 'Why do we keep having all these misunderstandings?'

'I don't know. Maybe it's because . . . '

Before she could finish her reply, Roberto bent down and kissed her. Then he smiled and whispered, 'That was so much better than squabbling, wasn't it?'

'Definitely,' Marina murmured, looking happily up at him, thinking, is this really happening?

'Let's do it again.' Roberto held her close, kissed her once more and said, 'Now I think it's time for some explanations.'

'Shall we have another drink first?'

'That's a good idea.'

Roberto released Marina, and she scuttled into the kitchen, glad to have a few moments away from Roberto to recover her breath. Just when she'd feared everything was over between them, he'd turned it all round and kissed her. That was unexpected. It seemed theirs was going to be a volatile relationship. If they were going to stay together, she would have to get used to that. Their personalities clashed, but if making up was always as good as just now, she wouldn't mind that.

She took their coffees into the lounge and discovered that Roberto was now sitting on the sofa, smiling and looking very relaxed.

'Come and sit beside me,' he urged.

She placed the cups on the table and sat down next to him.

'Do you want to go first?' Roberto asked. 'Let's hear your explanation.'

'Well, I haven't got much to tell,' Marina replied. 'I've told you about Jon already.'

'How is he?'

'He thinks his memory is coming back a little.'

'That's good isn't it?'

'Yes, but he . . . '

'Still thinks you and he are a couple. Is that it?'

'Yes. It's so difficult. I don't want to upset him, but it's hard pretending we're together. I wish I'd never agreed to do it in the first place.'

'But if, as you say, his memory is beginning to come back, he might soon remember for himself.'

'I suppose so.'

'Then he'll probably be really embarrassed when he realises.'

'He did say he was feeling embarrassed, but he said it was because he was still so dependent on everyone for help. Maybe you're right, though, and he is beginning to remember things about us.'

'It could be that. Why did you split up with him?'

'Well, Jon wanted to go to Australia. He thought it was a great opportunity, but I didn't want to go so far away, and I didn't want to leave Dad behind. I thought he was still grieving for Mum; as it's turned out, he obviously wasn't. He and Amelia are planning to move away from Mallory Wood. Did you know that?' Marina said bitterly.

'No I didn't. You really don't approve of your dad marrying Amelia, do you?'

'It just seemed so sudden. I never expected Dad to marry so soon.'

'Three years? Surely that's long enough to mourn for someone. How long should he have waited? They are both adults. They know what they're doing.'

'I hope so.'

'I gather you don't believe in love at first sight?' Roberto looked up at Marina.

'I don't know.' She hadn't believed in it — but since her father's wedding, she was beginning to wonder . . . 'Do you?'

'I do now.'

What did that mean? She quickly changed the subject.

'It's your turn for explanations, Roberto.'

'Okay, but there's not much to tell. I suppose you want to know about Rhoda.'

'Yes.'

'She's my business partner. She arranges exhibitions and tries to sell my pictures. I've known her for years, and she's very happily married. To someone else!'

'Thank you for telling me. Is there anything else I should know? What about Amelia?' She had to ask.

'Amelia?'

'How well do you know her?'

'Quite well. We grew up together. Went to the same school. We've been friends most of our lives.'

'Is that all?'

'Marina, what are you getting at?'

She could feel her face flushing.

'Are you implying that Amelia and I are more than just friends? Is that what you think?' Roberto stared at her.

'No. I just wondered if . . . '

'Amelia's in love with your Dad,' Roberto interrupted. 'Anyone can see that. Except you, it seems.'

'Yes, but . . . '

'No buts. I'm sure they will be very happy together.'

'What about the past?' Marina blurted out. She couldn't help herself. She had to know the answer. 'Were you and Amelia ever more than just friends?'

16

Marina arrived later than usual at the office the next day, after a restless night mulling over the events of the previous evening. She was normally very punctual, and was feeling annoyed with herself for oversleeping. She apologised to her boss and it was agreed she should stay late to get up to date with her work.

At lunchtime, Lionel came across to see her.

'Do you fancy going out to lunch?' he asked. 'It'd be nice to have a chat. I've got something to tell you.'

'I'm sorry to disappoint you, Dad. I really am too busy,' Marina replied, hardly glancing up at him. 'I can't talk now. I've got so much to do.' She was curious about what he had to say, though. 'Can I ring you one evening? You can tell me then.' She also knew he would want to hear about her meeting with Roberto. 'Now I must get on.'

'Okay. My news will keep,' Lionel sighed, and he wandered away.

Marina would have enjoyed being taken out for lunch, but didn't have any time to spare.

She was aware of several texts coming through on her mobile phone, but didn't look at them. She settled down and concentrated on her work.

She felt exhausted by the time she left the office, and bought a ready meal on the way home so she wouldn't need to spend long cooking.

After she had eaten, she looked at her phone. There were a couple of messages from friends, a text from Jon, and one from Roberto. She quickly looked at the ones from her friends, and then read Jon's message.

Come again soon, please Marina. There's so much we need to talk about. I'm trying hard to remember things, but everything is so muddled in my head. I need your help. You are the only one who can put me right. Love Jon.

Now what did that mean? Was his memory coming back? Was he remembering going to Australia? Or could it be that he was beginning to realise that they had split up, and was finding it hard to accept? Marina didn't know what to reply. She sat thinking for a few minutes and then sent the following text.

Very busy at work at the moment. I will let you know when I can come. I'm glad you are beginning to remember some things. Try not to worry too much. I will do what I can to help when I see you.

That was all true. Maybe this would be her opportunity to sort things out with him.

Then she read Roberto's message.

Hi Marina, I've calmed down now. I'm sorry I stormed off last night, but after explaining about Rhoda I didn't expect to be questioned about Amelia. We seem to lurch along from one crisis to another. Maybe we need to do some more talking. I will be free on Saturday. How would you like another day by the sea? Roberto.

He was right, Marina reflected. Life was certainly not smooth for them. Every time they seemed to be getting on well, something would happen to spoil things. This time though, Marina knew she was to blame for Roberto's outburst. She'd ruined everything by asking about any past relationship he might have had with Amelia. Why did she do it, she asked herself? He'd just explained about Rhoda. She should have kept quiet, but no, she'd blurted out, 'Were you and Amelia ever more than just friends?'

'What?' he'd exploded. 'More questions? It's late. I'm going home.'

'I'm sorry . . . ' she'd started to say, but Roberto marched over to the door.

'Goodnight,' he called, as he went out. 'Thanks for the coffee.'

She'd mulled over these events in bed the previous night, wondering if Roberto would contact her again. She was annoyed with herself. It was her fault the evening had ended that way; she seemed unable to control her tongue. It could have been so different. She was remembering the kisses they'd exchanged earlier. Why did she keep upsetting Roberto? She wasn't like this with anybody else. She decided that if there was any chance of them having a future together, she would have to try harder to think before speaking.

Then suddenly, it dawned on her — Roberto had ignored her question. He'd stormed off without answering. He could have denied being involved with Amelia if it wasn't true. Were her suspicions justified? Did it matter though, what he and Amelia had done in the past? Why did it bother her so much? Amelia was married to her father and they seemed happy enough.

Would she ever get an answer to her question? These thoughts whirled round in her head, causing a restless night.

Now she had to reply to Roberto's message. He'd been formal, so she would be too.

Apology accepted. Yes, I'd love to go to the coast on Saturday. Marina.

★ ★ ★

The next evening, she received a telephone call from Jon. His voice was low and husky. It had been like that when he'd first had the accident.

'Marina? I've got to talk to you.'

'Why? What's happened? Are you all right?' She was worried.

'I don't know.'

'What do you mean?'

'I'm remembering things.'

'That's good isn't it?'

'No.'

'It's what you wanted.'

'I don't like what I'm remembering. I keep hearing things in my head.'

'It will all get clearer in time.'

'I'm not sure.'

'Yes it will,' Marina tried to reassure him.

'I want to know something.'

'What's that?'

'Will you marry me, Marina?'

She wasn't expecting this now. She'd told Jon it was too soon after his accident to talk about it. She'd hoped his memory would come back and he'd say no more. What could she reply?

'I told you, it's too soon.'

'No, Marina, it isn't. We've known each other a long time.'

'Yes, but . . . '

'What's your answer?' he repeated.

'I . . . '

'You hesitated. The answer's no, isn't it, Marina? Tell me the truth.'

'It is. I can't marry you, Jon. I'm . . . '

'You're not in love with me. Was that what you were going to say?'

'Yes,' she murmured. 'I'm so sorry.'

'So am I.' He sounded distraught. 'These past few weeks have been awful, but the one bright spot was seeing you. I've been dreaming about us being together, but now those dreams are shattered. I had hoped you felt the same way about me.'

'Oh, Jon.' She felt terrible. 'I'm so sorry.'

'I just can't understand why you've been deceiving me all this time.'

What could she say to him?

'You can't deny it Marina,' he continued. 'You've been letting me believe that we were still together, letting me propose to you, not telling me that we'd gone our separate ways months ago. How could you do this to me, Marina?'

'I'm sorry, Jon. The doctors told me I wasn't to upset you.'

'I'm more than upset. I feel mortified.'

Marina had known right from the beginning that this might happen, but Jon's mother had convinced her to go along with him. She'd been wrong to agree.

'I'm sorry. What more can I say? I didn't want you to get hurt. The doctors said we had to be careful what we said. I can see now I should have explained things as soon as I saw you again.'

'Yes, you should. Then I would have known where I stood, and wouldn't have . . . let myself fall in love with you,' he quavered.

'Oh, Jon. I didn't want this to happen.'

'But it has.'

What could she say to Jon to make things better?

'I'm so sorry. I wish I'd been honest from the start, but everyone said I mustn't upset you. I was trying to do my best for you, but I . . . '

'Made everything worse,' Jon interrupted. 'I feel so stupid. I suppose my parents knew what was going on?'

'Yes. They thought we were doing the right thing too.'

'Well, you weren't,' Jon shouted. 'Goodbye, Marina. I shall never forgive you for what you did. I don't want to see you again.'

He hung up, and Marina burst into tears. She'd feared this might happen, but she'd given in to Jon's parents instead of following her own instincts. If only she hadn't listened to Barbara. It was too late now. Jon was devastated, and it was her fault. There was nothing else she could do.

*   *   *

Once again, Marina had a sleepless night. She lay in bed, running over the events of the last few weeks, wishing she'd acted differently. Since her father's wedding, she'd had nothing but trouble. The last thing she'd wanted was for Jon to fall in love with her. She'd been very fond of him and hated the thought of hurting him. She'd deceived him, and now they were both paying the penalty for it. She hoped he would soon get over her.

Then there was Roberto and her tempestuous relationship with him. She'd never expected to get so involved with someone after such a short time. Now, thoughts of him constantly filled her mind. Would she ever sort herself out?

★　★　★

Marina continued to be busy at work the next day, which she decided was a good thing. She had no time to dwell on her problems. There was a message from Barbara on her phone that she would have to deal with when she got home, but no word from Jon. She doubted he would ever contact her again; he was too upset and angry. She was sorry about that, and hated parting from him in that manner, but she knew there was no way she could make things better.

Roberto had also sent a text to say he was looking forward to the next day.

She replied that she was, too. She hoped that nothing would happen to spoil their day together.

When Marina arrived home from work, she phoned Barbara straight away.

'Jon's heartbroken,' his mother said accusingly. 'You could have let him down gently. Whatever did you say to him?'

'I didn't have to say much. He guessed . . . '

'He's in such a state,' Barbara interrupted. 'And it's all your fault.'

'That's not fair.' Marina tried to defend herself. 'I couldn't pretend any more. He remembered that we'd split up. I couldn't let him believe I was going to marry him, when that was never going to happen.'

'You didn't give him a chance.'

'I should have told him the truth when I first saw him after the accident. That was my mistake.'

'But the doctors said we shouldn't upset him.'

'I know, but it was wrong to keep the

truth from him. Jon was right. He said I had deceived him, and that's what we were all doing.'

'We just wanted to help him,' Barbara murmured forlornly.

'We did, but we got it wrong. He'll get over it.' Marina was trying to convince herself as well as Barbara. 'His memory's coming back. That's a good sign.'

'I hope so.'

Marina hung up, promising to ring again in a few days to see how Jon was. Then she telephoned her father.

'How's everything?' he enquired, before she could ask him what his news was.

'You mean, how did I get on with Roberto when I saw him?'

'Not just that. I want to know how you are. You looked very harassed when I saw you at work the other day.'

'Well, we have been extremely busy.'

'And Roberto?'

'He's okay. We are going out tomorrow.'

'That's very good. What about Jon? Any more news on him?'

Marina told her father about her conversations with him and Barbara.

'It's all very upsetting for everyone,' he commiserated.

'It is, but there's nothing I can do about it. Now, Dad, what have you got to tell me?'

'Something quite amazing.'

'What is it?'

'I still can't believe it.'

'Tell me,' Marina urged.

'Amelia's pregnant. You're going to have a baby step-brother or -sister.'

17

'Oh, Dad, I don't know what to say,' Marina gasped. 'I take it you're happy about it?'

'Yes. I'm feeling quite overwhelmed.'

'This is all so unexpected.'

'You are pleased, though, Marina?'

'Yes, of course Dad. It's just a bit of a shock.' Marina had never imagined this happening.

'It was for me too. At my age, I thought my child-rearing years were over.'

'You're not that ancient, Dad.'

'No, but I've forgotten how to deal with young children. After all it was twenty-five years ago that you were born.'

'It will all come back to you.'

'I suppose so.'

'And Amelia? What does she think about it?'

'She's delighted too.'

'Good.'

'So, I'll be calling on you to babysit.'

'I'd like that.'

'You'll have to get Roberto to help you.'

'I don't know about that. Anyway, we might not still be together.'

'Don't be so negative. It's time you settled down.'

'I'm not that old.'

'No, but I want you to be as happy as I am. Besides, I think Roberto would make a very good husband.'

'Oh, Dad,' Marina sighed. 'You don't know him very well, and you're looking too far into the future.'

'Maybe. But I don't think so. Anyway, I'd better go now and see how Amelia is. She hasn't been feeling very well.'

'Morning sickness, I suppose?'

'Yes, but it's not just in the morning. It's all day long. She's gone off her food and looks very pale, not like her old self at all.'

'She'll probably feel better after a few weeks.'

'I hope so. Also, I've been meaning to tell you that I'd put our house up for sale a few days ago, before we knew Amelia was pregnant, but I've phoned the agent and told them to take it off the market. We'll wait until after the baby is born now, see how we feel then. Amelia's in no fit state to have that worry.'

'You've done the right thing, Dad. You won't want to be miles from anywhere with a young baby. There's a lot going on for mums and babies in Mallory Wood.'

Marina couldn't help feeling glad he'd taken the house off the market. She hadn't been happy about them moving away into the country.

'That's what I've said to Amelia. You never know, after the birth I might be able to persuade her to stay.'

'I hope so. Besides, I'll be close at hand to babysit for you,' she added.

'That's what I thought. It might be

an incentive for her. Goodnight, Marina. Have a nice time tomorrow.'

'I'll try to. Goodnight, Dad.'

Marina hung up, feeling amazed. A baby brother or sister! That was completely unexpected. Yet it shouldn't have been. Amelia was only thirty-five. She should have realised this could happen. When Marina had been a child, she'd longed to have a brother or sister, but eventually she'd given up hope. Now, after all these years, it was actually going to happen — it was something of a shock.

★ ★ ★

The next morning, Roberto arrived early. Marina was ready for him, and they set off for the coast.

'You look nice,' he'd said, as he kissed her gently on the cheek.

The sun was shining as they reached Frinton.

'It's going to be a lovely day,' Roberto remarked, as he parked the car in a side-road. 'Let's find somewhere to have a coffee.'

'What's the news on Jon?' he asked, as they were sipping their drinks.

Marina recounted part of her telephone conversation with Jon, omitting the details of his proposal, and the fact that he had fallen in love with her.

'Oh, the poor chap! It must be so upsetting for him. I can't imagine how awful it must be, losing your memory for a time and then when it returns, finding everything is not as you expected.'

'That's right,' Marina replied. 'And I feel terrible for not telling him the truth sooner. He was furious with me for deceiving him.'

'But you were only trying to help.'

'He didn't see it that way.'

'No, I can understand that. It must have come as a shock to him.'

'That's right, but we were only doing what the doctors said, and trying not to upset him.'

'I guess Jon had become very

attached to you during those weeks of memory loss.' Roberto looked at Marina. 'He had probably fallen in love with you.'

She could feel herself blushing. What could she say? She couldn't deny it.

'Is that what happened?'

'Yes,' she murmured, not daring to look at Roberto.

'And you? How do you feel about him? Are you in love with Jon?'

'No. I never was.'

'That's good, then.'

'Is it?' Marina looked at Roberto.

'Of course.'

'Why?'

'I should think that's obvious.'

'Not to me.'

'Do I have to spell it out?'

'You do.' Marina held her breath. What was Roberto going to say?

'I don't make a habit of going out with girls who are in love with someone else.'

'Oh.' She didn't know what else to reply. That wasn't the answer she had hoped for. Then suddenly she blurted out, 'And how many girls have you been out with?'

'Enough to know what I'm looking for.'

'Have you found it?' Marina enquired, immediately wishing she hadn't asked.

Roberto gazed directly at her. 'Maybe. Maybe not. But we weren't discussing me. We were talking about Jon.'

Marina felt so embarrassed. Why did she say things without thinking?

'How's your painting going?' she asked quickly, changing the subject.

'Very well, thank you.'

'What are you working on?'

'Various things.' He finished his drink, looked at Marina and asked, 'Shall we walk along the beach?

* * *

After that tricky patch, the day passed pleasantly. The weather was fine, conversation flowed freely, and they both enjoyed their time by the sea.

In the evening, they had dinner in an attractive old inn.

'That was a lovely meal,' Marina said, as the waiter brought them coffee and mints.

'Yes, it was,' Roberto agreed. 'How's your dad?'

Marina cringed inside. Everything had been going so well. Now she would have to tell Roberto about Amelia, and she didn't know how he would react when he heard the news. But she had to tell him. If she didn't, he would think that she was deliberately keeping it from him.

'Dad's fine. He's actually in a bit of a daze, right now.'

'Why?' Roberto was looking concerned. 'What's wrong?'

'It's Amelia. She's pregnant.' There. She'd said it. Now what would he say?'

'That's wonderful!'

'It is?'

'Don't you think so?' Roberto was staring at her.

'Yes. It was just a bit of a shock.'

'What is it with you and Amelia? Every time she's mentioned, you look so disapproving. Can't you be pleased for them?'

'Of course I'm pleased. I just thought that . . . '

'I might not approve. Was that what you were thinking?'

He'd read her mind.

'Well . . . '

'Marina, can I tell you once more that I am delighted for Amelia. We have been friends since we were children, as I've told you before, and I know she will make a wonderful mother.'

'And that's all you have ever been? Just friends?' She had to ask. She needed to know. She was looking anxiously at Roberto.

'Okay, as that question seems to bother you so much, I'll give you an answer. Years ago, I did think we might one day settle down together, but Amelia had other ideas.'

'You were in love with her?'

'I thought so, at the time, but now I

realise it wasn't real love. We were both young, and she was very attractive. It was all so long ago. And Amelia was very ambitious. We both went to different universities, and things were never the same afterwards. She wanted someone who was going to do well in life, like your father. Not a struggling artist who earned his living as a paramedic. Within a few weeks of leaving university, she had met someone else and was married soon afterwards. I was very hurt at the time, but I got over it long ago.'

'I'd no idea Amelia had been married before. What happened?'

'The marriage didn't last, and she returned to live with her parents. Her husband was unfaithful to her and she divorced him.'

'And did she want to see you again?' Marina had to ask.

'Yes, but I'd learnt my lesson. I told her there was no future for us, and she accepted it. We managed to remain friends.'

So Marina had been right. She'd known there'd been something between them.

'And now?'

'Now we are still just good friends. How can I convince you that's all we are? Over the years, Amelia's had a few other boyfriends, but no one serious. She seemed reluctant to commit herself to anyone — until she met your dad.'

'Does my dad know that she has been married before?'

'I'm sure he does.'

'Why didn't he tell me?'

'I don't know. Perhaps he thought you would disapprove.'

'Is that what you think?'

'Well, you haven't been very enthusiastic about it.'

'I was just surprised by the speed of it all.'

'When you know you've found the right person, there's no point in waiting. That's how I see it.'

'Oh. You really think Amelia's in love with him? You don't think she married him for his . . . his . . . '

'I hope you weren't going to say 'money'.' Roberto's voice was sharp.

'Well, you said Amelia was ambitious.' Marina replied defensively.

'Yes — ambitious in her own right, for her own career. You seem to have such a low opinion of her,' Roberto snapped. 'You're completely wrong, though. She wouldn't do that.'

'I'm sorry. I just have my dad's best interests at heart.'

Roberto sighed. 'Here we go again, squabbling over Amelia. You have nothing to worry about. Your father will be quite safe with her.'

'I hope you're right.'

'I know I am. Now, do you believe that Amelia and I are just friends?'

'Yes, Roberto.' She had to say that. He'd believed her when she'd told him about Jon.

'So now that's all in the open, can we move on, please?'

Before Marina could reply, Roberto leaned across the table, took hold of her hand, kissed it and said, 'Let's try to have no more misunderstandings, please.'

'I'll try.'

'Good.'

They returned to Marina's flat. Roberto kissed her goodnight after making plans to see her the following weekend. 'I'm working extra shifts this week,' he told her. 'But we can go out next Saturday — if you're not heading off to Scotland.'

'Don't be so sarcastic. No, I won't be heading off to Scotland.'

'Okay. I can come over, pick you up and take you to my flat for lunch. I have something to show you. Would you like that?'

'I'd love it,' Marina answered. She'd wanted to see where he lived for ages. 'What have you got to show me?'

'You'll have to be patient and wait until next week.'

18

On Tuesday, Lionel caught up with Marina at work and asked if she would like to come over in the evening.

'Amelia will be pleased to see you. She's been feeling a bit sorry for herself the last few days. I'd forgotten how unpleasant morning sickness could be.'

'Yes, I'll come straight after work,' Marina promised. 'Dad, why didn't you tell me that Amelia had been married before?'

'Oh. I suppose Roberto told you?'

'Yes.'

'Well, I was going to, but never got round to it somehow.'

'I'd never suspected.'

'There was no reason why you should. Does it bother you then?'

'No, I was just surprised. Now I see why you didn't get married in a church. I had wondered.'

'She insisted that we should have the sound of wedding bells after the ceremony, though.'

'Yes, we heard them. Roberto's mother is a Catholic, too.'

'Yes, his mother and Amelia's parents attended church together, I think. We'll talk again tonight. I'd better get back to work. See you this evening.'

★ ★ ★

When Marina arrived at her dad's house, he let her in and told her to go into the lounge.

'Amelia's in there looking at all her baby books. Excuse me while I get on in the kitchen. Dinner won't be too long.'

Amelia, looking as beautiful as ever, despite being very pale, was seated on the sofa surrounded by cushions and magazines.

'Congratulations! How are you?' Marina asked, kissing her on the cheek.

'I feel awful, but at the same time

excited,' she replied.

'When's the baby due?'

'I've nearly seven months to wait. It's early days yet. Your dad's been marvellous though. He's really spoiling me.'

'That's good.'

'I'm such a lucky girl, marrying him. I really do love him, you know, in case you were wondering. The age difference doesn't matter to us. He's a lovely man, so kind and caring.'

'I'm glad.' What else could she say? Amelia had answered the question that had been worrying her for so long. Roberto had been right. Amelia was genuinely in love with her dad.

'Dinner will be ready in twenty minutes,' Lionel called from the kitchen.

'You seem to have got him well trained,' Marina remarked.

'He's had to be. I haven't been able to do much recently. I'm hoping this sickness will pass in a few weeks.'

'Yes, I'm sure it will,' Marina tried to reassure Amelia. 'Then you'll sail through the rest of your pregnancy.'

'I hope you're right. How's Roberto?' Amelia asked.

'He's okay.'

'I suppose he's told you that we grew up together. Our parents were friends. I've known him all my life.'

'Yes, he said that.'

'I want him to be as happy as I am. He's like a brother to me. It hasn't always been that way, but that was a long, long time ago. I hope you don't mind me telling you this.'

'No.'

'As your honorary step-mother,' Amelia continued, 'I feel I should say this. I think Roberto's serious about you, and I hope you feel the same way. I don't want him to be hurt again. Over the years, he's had a few romances, but none of them amounted to anything. I think his feelings for you are different. Do you understand what I'm trying to say?'

'Yes. I've no intention of hurting him, or anyone else.' Marina hadn't been expecting this. What had Roberto said to Amelia? Was it true that he was serious about her?

'Good,' Amelia continued. 'Now that's out in the open, we can be the best of friends.'

'That will be lovely,' Marina replied, suddenly realising she meant it. Her opinion of Amelia was changing for the better. She'd been wrong to be so suspicious. Her father and Roberto both trusted her, and she would do the same.

'There's one more thing,' Amelia continued. 'I don't know whether you've been told that this is my second marriage.'

'Yes, Roberto did mention it.'

'I was very young when I first got married. My husband was unfaithful to me and I divorced him.'

'I'm sorry. It must have been very hard for you.'

'Yes. It made me lose my confidence and trust in men. It's taken all these years for me to want to try again. A friend recommended I try a singles holiday. I was reluctant at first, but finally gave in, and amazingly, I met your father. He's a wonderful man. It was love at first sight, for both of us, but I expect your dad's told you all this.'

'Yes, he did say that.'

'I was so worried about meeting you, about how you would react to me — especially as I am closer to you in age than I am to your dad — but you have always been so welcoming and friendly, even though it must have been difficult for you. Also, I thought you might have resented the fact that I had been married before.'

Now Marina felt uncomfortable. Perhaps she wasn't such a bad actor after all — she certainly hadn't been very friendly or kindly disposed towards Amelia, but she obviously hadn't realised that. All that animosity Marina had thought was there was probably in her own mind.

'I was nervous about meeting you too,' Marina replied.

'Well, now we know where we stand there should be no more problems. And,' Amelia added, 'I hope you'll be able to help with the new baby.'

'I'd love that.'

'Dinner's ready,' Lionel called. 'Come on you two. I'm starving.'

★ ★ ★

When Marina arrived home that night there was a voicemail from Jon on her phone.

'I'm sorry I lost my temper with you the other day. My mother has convinced me that you were all trying to help. It's hard for me to see it that way, though, when I feel so let down about everything. It would be good if you felt able to ring me back. I think we do need to talk.'

Marina did so the following evening. 'How are you, Jon?'

'I feel terrible for the way I spoke to you. I'm so sorry.'

'Don't worry about it. I understand

why you were so angry. I realise now that we weren't helping you, but at the time, we thought we were doing the right thing.'

'And what you hadn't bargained for was me telling you that I'd fallen in love with you. Is that right?'

'Yes Jon. I'm so sorry. I didn't want that to happen.'

'It wasn't your fault. It was the unusual circumstances. I suppose there's no chance you will change your mind one day, is there? I really do love you, Marina. I don't know whether I did before I went to Australia, but I do now. I think about you all the time. Love can grow you know. If you gave me a chance . . .'

'No, Jon,' Marina interrupted. 'I won't change my mind. I like you as a friend, but that is all.' She didn't want to be unkind, but she couldn't give him false hope.

'I shouldn't have asked that,' Jon replied. 'Don't worry about me. I'll survive.'

'Thank you for being so understanding.'

'What else can I be? I've fallen in love with a pretty girl who doesn't feel the same way.' His voice faded away.

'I'm so sorry,' Marina whispered. She felt awful.

Suddenly Jon said, 'I've been so stupid. Why didn't I think of it before? Why would you want to stay with a man who's been disfigured and lost his memory? Is that what it is?'

'Jon, your injuries have never bothered me. Your injuries will get better and your memory will improve. I'm sure that, one day, you will meet someone else who will love you for who you are.'

'Have you met someone else? Is that why you don't want me? All this time, it never occurred to me that might have happened.'

'We're not discussing me.'

'That's given me my answer, I think. You have met someone else. Haven't you?'

'Everything will improve,' she answered, ignoring his question. She didn't know what else to say. 'You said yourself, your memory is improving and your scars will soon be gone.'

'Yes. The doctors think I will get back to normal in a few weeks now.'

'That's really good then.'

'I suppose so. You will keep in touch, Marina? Let me know how you are?'

'I will.'

'And I hope whoever it is you have met will make you very happy.'

'Thank you. And I hope you will be too, in time.'

Marina felt close to tears when she hung up. Poor Jon, she thought. Life hadn't been kind to him just recently. She genuinely hoped that things would start to get better for him.

And what of her future? What was in store for her? The weekend was fast approaching. How would her next encounter with Roberto go?

19

On Saturday morning, Roberto picked Marina up and drove her to his flat in East London. It was on the second floor of a modern tower block, overlooking a pleasant green and leafy square. As she walked through the front door, she noticed two large paintings hanging on the walls of the very spacious entrance hall.

She stopped and gazed up at one of them.

'What a beautiful picture. You painted it? It's so realistic, you almost feel as if you're there, standing by the lake, looking across to the mountains.'

'Yes. I painted it from a photograph I took when I was on holiday in Scotland, some years ago.'

Marina looked up at the second picture depicting cliffs and the sea.

'That's lovely, too. I can see why you

want to be an artist. You're brilliant at painting.'

'Thank you, but you've only seen two of my works. You might have a different opinion when you see some others.'

'I'm sure I won't. I'm most impressed.'

'Come into the lounge and make yourself comfortable.'

Marina gazed around, amazed by the charm and elegance of the room, which was enhanced by the colourful land-scapes and seascapes adorning the walls.

'I love your flat. It's just perfect.'

'You sound surprised,' Roberto said. 'I suppose you expected a typical bachelor flat, sparsely furnished, but as you can see, I like my comfort.'

'I wasn't sure what to expect. After all, we don't know each other very well.'

'Not yet, but I think that can be remedied.'

'Can it?'

'I hope so.'

Roberto was staring intently at Marina. She smiled shyly, and he moved across the room.

'Now might be a good time to start,' he said, taking her into his arms and kissing her, gently at first and then becoming more passionate as she responded to him.

'How was that?' he whispered as they paused for breath.

'Wonderful,' she breathed.

'Now do you think we know each other better?'

'A little.'

Roberto laughed and pulled away. 'That's enough for now. I'm going to make us a coffee. Then I'll show you my studio.'

Marina sank down onto the sofa in a daze. No one had ever had this effect on her before. She was feeling completely overwhelmed by Roberto.

By the time he returned with their coffees Marina had recovered herself. They sat drinking and chatting amicably about her job and his work as a paramedic. When they had finished she asked, 'Can I see your studio now?'

'Of course. Follow me.'

Roberto's flat was bigger than she expected. He led her back to the entrance hall, and to the far end of the corridor.

'Here we are,' he said, as he opened the door into a large room with an easel in the middle and a plethora of paintings stacked along the walls. As she looked at the easel she gasped.

'Mallory Wood!'

'That was what I wanted to show you. I painted it after you took me there. Do you like it?'

'It's beautiful. I love it.' She gazed at it in wonder. 'You're so talented.'

'I'm glad you like it. I'm quite pleased with it. You can have it. We'll take it back tonight.'

'Are you sure? You don't want to keep it yourself or exhibit it? You could even sell it.'

'No. I painted it for you.'

'Thank you, Roberto. It's the best present I've ever had.' Tears streamed down her face.

He rushed over and put his arms around her. 'What's the matter? Don't cry, Marina.'

'I'm just so happy,' she smiled as she reached up and kissed him.

'Can I look at some of your other pictures please?' she asked a few minutes later.

They spent the next hour examining his other works of art. He explained what the pictures were, and why he'd painted them. He then took her into an adjoining room, where he had his photographic studio.

'I'm so impressed,' she said, when they'd finished looking at everything. 'I hadn't realised I was going out with a great artist and photographer.'

'I'm not that, but I am beginning to have some success with my work. That was what I was going to tell you. Rhoda set up an exhibition for me, and we managed to sell quite a few of my paintings, for a lot more money than I expected. And I have some commissions too. A couple of businessmen have asked me to do paintings for their boardrooms, and they will pay very well if they are satisfied.'

'Oh, Roberto, that's marvellous.'

'I also have a couple of bookings for photo shoots, so I hope that will take off too. It's what I've always dreamed about, but never thought would happen.'

'I'm so pleased for you. You're going to be very busy.'

'It looks like it.'

'So, will you give up your work as a paramedic?'

'Not yet. Perhaps I will one day though. I still enjoy it. It's hard work, but when I've finished a shift I feel as if I have achieved something worthwhile. I've helped someone, maybe saved their life.'

'That must be a wonderful feeling.'

'It is. I suppose that's why I'm reluctant to give it up.'

'Could you do it part time?'

'If my art really takes off, which seems likely at the moment, I will look into doing that. I don't know what my father will have to say about all this though; it's not what he had in mind for me at all.'

'I'm sure he will be delighted when he hears how successful you are.'

'I don't know about that. Maybe I'll have some other news for him too, the next time I see him.'

'What's that?'

'It's time for lunch,' Roberto said, ignoring Marina's question. 'Let's head out.'

The afternoon passed happily. There were no silly squabbles, and both got on perfectly.

'Can we go back to Mallory Wood later?' Roberto asked. 'I'd like to see it once again.'

'Yes, and maybe you can take some more photos.'

'I suppose you want me to paint another picture for you,' Roberto smiled.

'Not for me. I was thinking maybe you could do one for your parents. It might make your dad more interested in your art.'

'That's a good idea. I'll do it. Shall we have dinner at the restaurant we visited before?'

'Yes, please.'

* * *

They returned to Mallory Wood early in the evening. As before, the sun was shining, bathing everywhere in a golden light. They walked past the lake, and paused once again to admire the view which Roberto had painted.

'Henry the Eighth had good taste coming here,' Roberto remarked.

'Yes, it's a lovely spot,' Marina agreed.

'This has been a perfect day,' Roberto said, as they sat down on a bench overlooking the lake. He put his arm around her and they watched the ducks and geese cavorting about.

'It has, 'Marina replied, snuggling up to him. 'I don't want it to end.'

'There will be plenty more wonderful days, I hope.'

'Will there?'

'That depends on you.'

'What do you mean?'

'I've been debating with myself when to say this — whether it was too soon — but now, I don't think I can wait any longer.'

'What do you want to say?' Marina was looking at Roberto anxiously.

'I think you can guess.'

'No. Tell me.'

He pulled her closer and looked into her eyes.

'I've fallen in love with you, Marina. I've been wondering how to tell you and what your reaction would be.'

'Oh Roberto, I love you too.'

'You do?'

'Yes,' she whispered.

'I can't believe this has happened,' Roberto murmured, kissing her passionately until they were both breathless. 'I never thought I'd feel this way. Ever since the day I met you, I haven't been able to get you out of my mind. I suppose I was a rather reluctant wedding guest, as I know you were. I was pleased for Amelia in one way, but at the same time I couldn't help being a little bit jealous of how happy they both were. Then I saw you, and all those feelings vanished. It was love at first sight. I didn't believe in it until I met you.'

'Oh, Roberto, I never guessed. I thought you found me irritating.'

'I knew I was attracted to you, but I didn't want to be. I was afraid of getting hurt again. Anyway, you told me I was pompous, so I was amazed when you agreed to go out with me.'

'And I was surprised when you asked me to. So many misunderstandings!' Marina sighed.

'Yes, and many others since that day. But from now onwards, let's hope there will be no more.'

'We can try. I felt the same way. I was attracted to you, but was not at my best that day. My dad's wedding was the last place I ever expected to meet anyone. I resented him getting married and was opposed to Amelia from the start.'

'And now?'

'You and Amelia have convinced me that I was wrong. Dad's entitled to be happy again, and I can see they're both in love, so I'm sure it will work out, especially now she's pregnant.'

'I think it will.'

'Dad told me he had fallen in love with Amelia at first sight, and that it would happen to me one day, but I didn't believe him. He was right though. From the moment I first saw you looking across at me at the wedding ceremony, my life changed. You have constantly been in my thoughts, but I hardly dared hope you would feel the same. Then there was all the upset with Jon and . . . '

'I didn't make it easy for you,' Roberto interrupted. 'I was jealous of all the time and attention you were giving to him. I should have had more compassion. After all, you were only trying to help. It's my job, helping people, but all I could think about was that you were with him. You see what sort of person I am, Marina. It's my temperament — I can be hasty. Are you sure you still want to get involved with me?'

'Yes, Roberto. I have never been more sure of anything in my life.'

'Oh, Marina,' he murmured, kissing her again.

'I did understand why you resented me spending time with Jon,' she said, a few minutes later. 'But I couldn't just abandon him. I felt I had to help, in any way I could.'

'And you did the right thing. I was just being selfish.' Roberto took hold of her hands. 'There's one more thing I want to ask you.'

'What's that?'

'I know we haven't been together very long, but I'm sure you are the only girl for me. Marina, will you marry me?'

'Oh, yes please, Roberto.' Tears streamed down her face.

'We can spend the rest of our lives

getting to know each other.' He pulled her close and kissed her again.

'The money from the sale of my pictures will come in very handy now there's a wedding to plan. Marina — what do you think about buying a house in Mallory Wood?'

'I'd love that.'

'And what about our honeymoon? Where shall we go?'

'I don't mind, as long as I am with you.'

'Well, how would you like to go to Italy? We could tour around, spend some time on our own, and then maybe visit some of my relatives? I'm sure they would love to meet you.'

'That sounds wonderful. You've got everything planned, Roberto.'

'If you don't like my ideas, you don't have to agree.' He looked at Marina anxiously.

'I love them, Roberto.'

'I have other plans too, which I hope you will like.'

'What are they?'

'In a couple of years' time, I hope your father will be a grandfather, as well as a new dad. Italians love children. What do you say, Marina?'

She blushed, but couldn't help smiling. 'I think your plans are just perfect, Roberto.'

'Shall we tell your dad tomorrow? I'm not working then.'

'Yes. I know he'll be pleased.'

'I think Amelia will be too.'

'What about your parents, Roberto?'

'I'll ring them. We'll make arrangements to go and visit them very soon. They'll be delighted. They keep telling me it's time I settled down. But I always reply that I'm waiting for the right girl to come along.' He gazed into her eyes, kissed her and whispered, 'And now, at last, she's here.'

A few minutes later, he released her and said, 'I think it's time we had dinner. I've suddenly got an enormous appetite.'

'So have I. But there's just one more thing, Roberto.'

'What's that?'

'Can we have real wedding bells at our wedding?'

'I wouldn't have it any other way.'

'Thank you, Roberto.'

He took her hand, and they walked forward, dreaming of their wonderful life ahead.

Other titles in the
Linford Romance Library:

CHRISTMAS REVELATIONS

Jill Barry

Reluctant 1920s debutante Annabel prefers horses to suitors. When she tumbles into the path of Lawrence, Lord Lassiter, she's annoyed that this attractive man is the despised thirteenth guest joining her family for Christmas — for he has been involved in a recent scandal, and only he and his faithful valet, Norman Bassett, know the truth behind the gossip. Meanwhile, as Lawrence tries to charm Annabel, Norman has a surprise encounter with a figure from his past — one who has been keeping a secret from him for years . . .

WHERE THE HEART LIES

Sheila Spencer-Smith

Amy sets off to join her wildlife photographer boyfriend Mark on the Isles of Scilly, accompanied by her sister's dog Rufus, who she is dropping off with her sister's parents-in-law, Jim and Maria, at Penmarrow Caravan Site. But when she arrives, the park is deserted — except for the handsome Callum Savernack, who doesn't appear happy to have her there. When it emerges that Jim and Maria are temporarily unable to return to Penmarrow, Amy finds herself torn between her responsibilities to Mark, to Rufus — and to Callum . . .

THE SHADOW IN THE DARK

Susan Udy

Attempting to escape the scandal that has engulfed her, Daisy Lewis leaves home and heads for the Cornish town of Pencarrow, still as beautiful as she remembers from her childhood holidays. But news spreads like wildfire in the small, tightly knit community, and soon she must deal with a blackmailer who recognises her from her previous life. Even worse, she suspects it could be one of the two handsome men who are keen to romance her. Is there anyone Daisy can trust — and will her secret be exposed yet again?

ENCHANTMENT IN MOROCCO

Madeleine McDonald

Stranded in Morocco, Emily Ryan accepts a job offer from a stranger. Entranced by her new life in the sleepy coastal village of Taghar, she struggles to resist widower Rafi Hassan's charm — but also clashes with his autocratic ways and respect for tradition. As she attempts to persuade him to allow his teenage daughter Nour more freedom, Emily refuses to acknowledge her own errors of judgement. As the seasons turn and the olives ripen, Emily dares to dream of winning Rafi's heart — until danger threatens from an unexpected quarter . . .

NO TIME FOR SECOND BEST

Jo Bartlett

When Ellie Chapman finds out that she's inherited her Great-aunt Hilary's farm on the beautiful Kentish coast, and is then made redundant from her office job, it looks like life has handed her the new start she's been craving. But there are choppy waters ahead, from difficulties with her ex-fiancé, to the unexpectedly dilapidated state of the farm, to a menagerie with a poorly donkey and a wayward sheep. Love is waiting in the wings for both Ellie and her mum, however, as well as some exciting new opportunities . . .